YOGA
FOR ALL

Hansaji J. Yogendra, a charismatic personality, is the director of The Yoga Institute, the world's oldest organized yoga centre. She is the leading face of householder yoga and has transformed the lives of millions by conducting free counselling sessions as well as over one lakh theoretical and practical sessions of yoga till date. Being at the forefront of the yoga fraternity for over five decades, her significant contributions in areas like yoga education, research, experiential learning, standardization of yoga practices, upliftment of society, communication via television/digital medium as well as numerous books authored by her have been widely recognized. She has headed significant research projects, reports of which have been published in various forms. She also serves as a yoga expert to many prestigious organizations and government committees and has bagged numerous awards and accolades. She has brought about key revolutionary changes in the field of yoga by spreading yoga education especially for women. An inspiring teacher, she remains a beacon of hope and a messenger of goodwill to millions from all over the world who flock to the institute to learn yoga under her guidance. Hansaji is the only lady yoga guru conferred with the privilege of sharing the dais with Prime Minister Narendra Modi on the first International Yoga Day on 21 June 2015.

YOGA FOR ALL

Discovering the true essence of yoga

Hansaji J. Yogendra

ESTD 1918
The Yoga Institute
WORLD HARMONY BEGINS WITHIN

RUPA

Published by
Rupa Publications India Pvt. Ltd 2018
7/16, Ansari Road, Daryaganj
New Delhi 110002

Sales centres:
Allahabad Bengaluru Chennai
Hyderabad Jaipur Kathmandu
Kolkata Mumbai

Copyright © The Yoga Institute 2018
Edited by Damini Dalal

The views and opinions expressed in this book are the
author's own and the facts are as reported by him which
have been verified to the extent possible, and the publishers
are not in any way liable for the same.

ISBN: 978-93-5304-085-7

Fourth impression 2019

10 9 8 7 6 5 4

The moral right of the author has been asserted.

Printed at Parksons Graphics Pvt. Ltd, Mumbai

CONTENTS

FOREWORD

Our bodies are our temple. We should always endeavour to keep it pure and clean for the soul to reside in. Most of us have absolutely no idea how good our bodies are designed to feel. I believe that the greatest gift you can give your family and the world is a healthy you. When one listens to oneself, everything comes naturally—from inside, like an addition of energy, strength and beauty to body, mind and soul—which is yoga. Anyone who practices can obtain success in yoga. Constant practice alone is the secret to success.

This classic book *Yoga for All* is a humble recognition of the need in modern society for guidance towards a way of living that is in greater harmony with our natural surroundings and more synergistic with our fellow beings.

I extend my admiration, gratitude and best wishes to all who have contributed so painstakingly through this book, in carving out a path that is for the betterment of mankind.

Amitabh Bachchan

PREFACE

The world over, health is discussed under several dimensions: physical, emotional, sensual, intellectual, ethical and spiritual. Yoga plays an all-inclusive role where the person is considered in totality and not in isolation of any particular characteristics.

Today, the terms yoga and asana have become synonymous and a whole physical culture has arisen devoid of the beautiful facets of its founding philosophy. To re-envision and transform the trend, this book brings back the freshness and wholesomeness to the traditional techniques of yoga and views them in their myriad dimensions.

Within the pages of this book, Hansaji J. Yogendra, has brought forth her immense experience over decades of practice and teaching yoga into a concise and systematic format, integrating the ancient wisdom into the traditional practices. She has introduced multiple variations to the postures to include all levels of yoga enthusiasts. These variations are useful to both the beginner as well as the advanced practitioner of yoga.

Practices designed by her called Sahaj Bhavasanas have been discussed in detail in the book. The practices of The Yoga Institute are described in the chapter The Unique Practices of The Yoga Institute. Different asanas, pranayamas and kriyas are discussed in separate chapters. There is a special chapter on facial yoga called 'Forever Young.'

The book introduces foundational philosophical ideas from the ancient Samkhya philosophy of Ishvara Krishna. The integration of ethical and spiritual values within the physical practices of yoga is the exceptional contribution of Dr Jayadeva Yogendra, former president of The Yoga Institute. These concepts known as the bhavas are interwoven in a manner such that each yoga technique when practised, induces a corresponding psychological and spiritual effect.

Prior to commencing the practices, it is desirable that the reader reads and reflects upon the glorious traditions of yoga briefly explained in the first chapter. This will bring about a new perspective and experience, way beyond any physical practice alone.

This book integrates a timeless, value-based philosophy into the techniques of yoga, making it a unique contribution to the treasures of yoga treatises.

Wishing you a successful journey on the path of yoga!

Damini Dalal,
The Yoga Institute,
Mumbai

IN GRATITUDE

In November 2016, Hansaji J. Yogendra entrusted me with a brief: to compile a book on asanas and to integrate the values of The Yoga Institute and the philosophy of Samkhya within the practices. I am grateful for her faith in me. I feel truly blessed to have sat with her so often, discussing the finer nuances of the philosophy, the yoga practices and integrating her wisdom in this book.

After commencing work, I soon realized this was an immense task, as this book would have to stand apart from the numerous other books on asanas flooding the market by integrating an ancient philosophy within the practices. My task, though seemingly easy, was complex.

However, my assignment flowed seamlessly as a team of senior yoga teachers, Nishi Tataria and Mohan Ramaswami, provided the initial format.

Sharad Chauhan's erudite writings inspired the affirmations to the practices along with conversations with Dilipbhai Tralshawala and Kartik Vyasa, both senior sadhakas of The Yoga Institute and dynamic yoga teacher, Deepa Thukral.

I am grateful to Prema Parab and Latika Kurup who assisted in formatting the manuscript, Aradhana Vaishnav for the initial proofreading, Amrita Sharma for her research on the benefits of the practices, Vrutti Karia for assimilating the photographs into the manuscript. Thanks to Dr Atul Pednekar for his medical expertise.

I thank the models, Pramila Khubchandani and Samarth Jani, both trained teachers of The Yoga Institute, along with Nirali Manek, photographer and her team to have brought alive the yoga practices.

Finally, I would extend my gratitude to Jyotsna Mehta, senior editor, Rupa Publications, for her invaluable suggestions.

Damini Dalal

OUR LEGACY

The Yoga Institute was founded on 25 December 1918 by Yogendraji. It found a permanent base in Santacruz, Bombay (now Mumbai), in 1948. Spread over an acre of land amidst Nature, with three buildings dedicated to yogic activities, this non-profit organization has been running on its own strength for almost ten decades. It entered its 100th year on 25 December in 2017. Thousands of people visit the institute every day for training and health consultations.

PARAMHAMSA MADHAVADASJI—
GURU OF FOUNDER SHRI YOGENDRAJI

His Holiness Paramhamsa Madhavadasji was born in 1798 to a Mukhopadhyaya family in Bengal. His upbringing inspired in him a devotional attitude. At the tender age of twenty-three, he left his home in search of higher pursuits whilst working as a lawyer. His early association with bhakti rituals could not satisfy the reformist concepts that he was seeking, so he learnt different traditions by travelling across Assam, Tibet and the Himalayas to get a first-hand knowledge of yoga. In his later years, Paramhamsa Madhavadasji was in Bombay at Madhavbaug for a discourse where he met Yogendraji (then known as Mani). A strong bond developed between the two, and he personally guided and trained Mani on the path of yoga.

FOUNDER—YOGENDRAJI

Yogendraji was born as Mani Haribhai Desai in 1897 in Gujarat. Through a chance meeting, he found his guru, Paramhamsa Madhavadasji and learnt all about yoga from him. With the blessings of his guru, Yogendraji went on to spread the esoteric knowledge of yoga among the masses, as he felt it could greatly improve the lives of people. He founded The Yoga Institute at 'The Sands', the residence of Dadabhai Naoroji in Versova in 1918.

There, he helped many people recover from various ailments through yoga. Following this, he travelled to the United States and founded The Yoga Institute in Harriman, New York, in 1920, where he undertook much research on the subtle physiological and psychological effects of yoga along with scientists and doctors. Yogendraji then returned to India and following the wishes of his father, married and remained a 'Householder Yogi'. He has written many authoritative texts on yoga based on the ancient scriptures. Some of his books are even preserved in the Crypt of Civilization for posterity. Along with his wife, Sitadevi, Yogendra continued to teach and spread the awareness of classical yoga at the institute until his passing away in 1989.

SITADEVI YOGENDRA

Sitadevi Yogendra, fondly known as Mother, married Yogendraji in 1927 and joined him in his mission to spread the knowledge of yoga. She began teaching women and children at the institute and has written many articles and books on the subject. Her book, *Yoga: Physical Education for Women* is also preserved in the Crypt of Civilization. Mother Sitadevi passed away in 2008 at the age of ninety-seven.

DR JAYADEVA YOGENDRA—PRESIDENT OF THE YOGA INSTITUTE

Born in 1929, son of Yogendraji and Sitadevi, Dr Jayadeva Yogendra was a simple man and a true yogi. Having seen his complete dedication to a life of discipline and simplicity, the sadhakas (disciples) of the institute consider him as their true guru. Being born in a family of yogis, he had a spiritual inclination since childhood. As the president of The Yoga Institute, he continued the founder's legacy with utmost sincerity. He was also the editor of the institute's monthly journal, *Yoga & Total Health* published since 1933.

Dr Jayadeva had completed his master's in Samkhya philosophy and yoga at Bombay University in 1952.

In 1955, he was awarded the Har Gobind scholarship for a PhD for his thesis on Moksha Parva. He had introduced several courses at the institute, and had done pioneering work in yoga education and therapeutics. Students at the institute drew inspiration from his wisdom, compassion, wit and unflinching commitment to truth.

HANSAJI JAYADEVA YOGENDRA—
DIRECTOR OF THE YOGA INSTITUTE

A dynamic and charismatic personality, Hansaji, wife of Dr Jayadeva Yogendra and the present director of the Yoga Institute, has dedicated her life to its running and teaching yoga as a way of life in a completely practical way. She was honoured as the 'Woman of the Year 2000' by the American Biographical Institute, for her outstanding accomplishments and being the noble example for our society. She is perhaps best known for the popular television series *Yoga for Better Living,* first aired in 1980.

Hansaji was recognized for her contribution to women's health through the award presented by the Society for the Promotion of Area Resource Centers (SPARC). She has conducted several seminars and lecture tours in India and Europe, Australia, Canada, Pakistan, Hong Kong and the US. She has also authored many books and articles on yoga. She was invited by the National Council for Education Research and Training (NCERT) along with Dr Jayadeva to formulate a syllabus focusing on yoga for schools nationwide.

HOW TO USE THIS BOOK

A HOLISTIC APPROACH

For a holistic approach and to acquire benefits at all levels through the practice of yoga (the practices described in this book), it is best that you read the entire book prior to practice.

The aim is to understand how associated thoughts need to be cultivated and infused with the physical yoga practices for a unified experience.

All the practices commence with a thought to be inculcated during practice, which is to be extended into life and living.

DIFFERENT SECTIONS AND CHAPTERS

Introduction

The introduction to the Samkhya philosophy behind the practices is supplemented with a comprehensive understanding of the several facets that will transform the way you practise yoga and make it into an inspiring and enriching experience.

Sahaj Bhavasanas by Hansaji J. Yogendra

Hansaji J. Yogendra, over several decades of teaching yoga recognized the need to modify several traditional postures such that every person can take benefit of the practices. She firmly believes that yoga is for all and not for the few, slim and flexible people. Becoming self-reliant (svavalambi) and to desire to remain healthy and fit to perform one's duty towards oneself, family and then society is vital.

Thus several of her postures can be done sitting or even lying down. Many can be done by the ill and the aged. Yoga is for every individual irrespective of gender, body type or age. There is something for everyone!

With reference to the needs of the current generation some variations are especially designed to benefit the sedentary lifestyles of desk personnel who are continuously slumped in front of their computers.

Asanas

Major types of asanas discussed: meditative, cultural, relaxation, along with Hansaji's variations.

Each asana has a breathing rhythm to be practised during its performance. The details are given in the chapter on pranayamas.

Pranayamas

There is an introduction to the concept of prana and detailed instructions to the practice of Yogendra Pranayamas and traditional pranayamas.

Unique Practices of The Yoga Institute

At The Yoga Institute, the main focus is on the 'householder'. A householder is any person who takes care of the self, earns a livelihood, looks after the family and actively participates in family and social activities as fundamental duties. 'Householder' refers to every person living in society, irrespective of whether one is married, lives alone or with a partner, has children or otherwise. No one is beyond the scope of the definition.

The Yoga Institute is a life school. Keeping in mind the problems and needs of the common person, these techniques seek to inculcate a deep transformation within the psyche. They are seemingly simple but profound in their effects!

Kriyas

Institutional and traditional kriyas are explained simply and clearly for ease of practice.

The Symbols

Stars are given next to the name of the asana. They represent the ease or difficulty of practice.

* Beginner's level
** Intermediate level
*** Advanced level

The practices marked with a single or double stars are important for the advanced practitioner as well.

Most of the Sahaj Bhavasanas can be practised by all. In case of difficulty, they will be marked with double stars.

As a beginner, you can choose to practise in stages or omit a few asanas. You can also choose to practise fewer numbers of repetitions. The idea is to go slowly but steadily without injuring yourself.

As an advanced practitioner, you can increase the number of repetitions. Being focused and static in some of the asanas will give you experiences of another dimension rather than merely going through the whole series mechanically and fast.

With this in mind, let us commence on this enriching journey of wellness of the body, mind and spirit!

1

BHAVAS AND YOGA

WHAT IS YOGA?

An age-old question always arises about what is yoga? Every yoga teacher is frequently asked which form of yoga they practise or teach. There are no simple answers. Today, yoga is often equated with physical practices such as asanas, pranayamas, kriyas and so forth. Its philosophy is often neglected completely. Devoid of a philosophical base, such physical practices can very well be any other form of exercise.

It is said in the classical Hatha Yoga text, *Hatha Yoga Pradipika*, that Hatha Yoga is to be practised for the purpose of Raja Yoga alone (kevalam rajayogaya), that is, for psychological evolution and spiritual ascent. The physical benefits such as removal and alleviation of diseases, good health and slimness of body are all its by-products.

There are several forms of yoga. Some have become very popular. However, a great deal of ambiguity in traditional texts gave way to the multiplicity of interpretations. Raja, Tantra, Mantra, Laya, Hatha are the several more forms of yoga. These have been greatly modified today and due to the guru-shishya parampara (guru-disciple lineage) some of these practices carry the names of their respective gurus.

Yoga is derived from the Sanskrit word 'yuj'. Diverse ideas of 'yuj' are given in the different scriptural texts; for instance, union or joining, reaching the highest state of absolute concentration (samadhi) as well as the ability to control the senses (samyama).

However, yoga is an all-encompassing term. It represents the means, the path and the end. It includes the entire person within its purview: the body, mind (emotions), intellect and consciousness (which has been the subject of much study and debate in both the philosophical world as well as the scientific community).

In this book, a detailed discussion on what is yoga is avoided to eliminate confusion between its practices and different philosophical interpretations, as Indian philosophy has grown over centuries and its study is exceptionally multifaceted.

At The Yoga Institute, the physical practices of yoga have been interwoven with specific philosophical ideas. The next section briefly explains the concepts from one of the oldest philosophical schools, Samkhya.

SAMKHYA PHILOSOPHY AND THE CONCEPT OF BHAVA

The Yoga Institute is the only yoga institute in the world where the techniques of yoga are practised and understood in relation to and integrated with the ancient Samkhya philosophical principles of the 'bhavas'. This is an initiative by Dr Jayadeva.

In Indian philosophy, the term 'bhava' is used widely. It is often loosely translated as an emotion or feeling and its expression. Philosophically it means the inherent and intrinsic nature of a thing or entity—its predisposition. For instance, the bhava of glass is to break whereas the bhava of steel is unbreakable.

A person can be predisposed to, or possess, for example, the bhavas of love, anger, greed, meekness, or incompetence. The list would be long! For example, people are described as having bhakti bhava (predisposition to devotion), karuna bhava (compassion), bhava of revenge and an endless number of such mental states which may be contradictory too.

An important feature of bhava is its capacity to undergo transformation.

Indian philosophy believes that there is an inherent purpose in the existence of things, and this purpose is the evolution of human consciousness to its fullest potential.

However, it is the application of its philosophical principles in day-to-day life where we realize that Indian philosophy and its practice are interwoven like the warp and weft of a fabric with innumerable patterns that culminate in a beautiful whole.

THE SAMKHYA KARIKAS AND THE NOTION OF BHAVA

Samkhya is one of the six classical Indian philosophical systems known as the Shad Darshana. Though the founding rishi is sage Kapila, the Samkhya karikas (verses on Samkhya) of Ishvara Krishna form the basis of current Samkhya study. The philosophical principles of Samkhya and the techniques of yoga form a cohesive and unified whole. The karikas are a philosophical exposition on life, living and liberation.

All individuals at any stage in life possess certain qualities which may or may not be conducive to self-development. These form their basic nature or bhava. The Samkhya karikas enumerate four bhavas to be cultivated by a person on the path of personal growth. These represent your inherent potential. The karikas also imply four negative traits that lead to a deluded state of mind.

The karikas encourage the practice and development of the four bhavas of dharma, jnana, vairagya (viraga) and aishvarya, which encourage an individual towards personal growth. They discourage the practice of the four negative bhavas. These eight bhavas are characteristics of buddhi, the cognitive, affective, conative and retentive faculty of human beings. The bhavas enable you to recognize your potential for positive growth as well as to identify fallacies and take a twofold mode of action. Such action is firstly to introduce the practice of the four positive bhavas and simultaneously to reduce the four negative bhavas of adharma, ajnana, raga and anaishvarya.

THE FOUR DESIRABLE AND CONSTRUCTIVE BHAVAS

The bhavas are inner principles to be practised by an individual for self-development and not general instructions or societal rules.

Dharma Bhava

This bhava represents what you ought to do. It is the foundational predisposition. The entire structure of human potential and development rests on it.

Dharma bhava is multifaceted and its fundamental principle is duty, which is a powerful word, including righteous conduct, developing steadiness and leading towards a spiritual goal.

In yoga, the first duty is towards oneself. It is not selfish but primary as only a person fit of body and mind can perform positive actions.

Dharma bhava involves taking responsibility for all of your actions through self-discipline and self-motivation. All other bhavas fall in step, such that without the practice of dharma, the other bhavas become insignificant.

This bhava leads to a fulfilling and enriching life. Dharma bhava rises above pettiness. It creates a balanced state of mind. Maintaining equipoise, while doing any activity is dharma.

All actions henceforth are not mere reactions but conscious knowledge-based actions.

The word 'dharma' is not to be confused with the word 'religion'. Dharma is the personal principle of transformative behavioural and attitudinal dispositions.

Jnana Bhava

Through the practice of dharma, jnana arises. Keen awareness and realization unfolds as you become more fine-tuned to your actions and relations to the world outside.

The development that occurs through the practice of dharma ensures the development of jnana, knowledge of your body–mind relationship. Such knowledge in turn helps in understanding how to manage the outside world through inner knowledge-based transformations. It is discriminative knowledge which allows you to make independent and informed choices.

Jnana is to develop one-pointedness. It is increasing concentration and focus while doing any activity. It is the bhava through which mindfulness and self-awareness develop and such awareness transforms all activities in relation to the self and the world. This represents the predominant feature of the conscious mind.

Thus, jnana represents awareness and wisdom and not mere informative knowledge of the world.

Vairagya (Viraga) Bhava

Objectivity is the central idea of vairagya. Often misunderstood as relinquishment of the activities and beauty of life, it is more about a 'mind-state' that is beyond greed and personal attachments that bind you into endless misery. It is to refrain from accumulating a mountain of thoughts that form a formidable baggage. Vairagya also inhibits excessive hoarding of material possessions.

The essence in vairagya is letting go of all the pettiness and useless cravings that persist in the mind. It is the principle of non-attachment that accepts the world as it is, performs actions whenever and whatever is needed according to one's capacities. It allows a peaceful existence in the world without causing undue stress to oneself or others, resulting in a larger perspective of life.

Humility manifests as there is no arrogance of knowledge, power or position, rather it ensures an objective and impartial state of mind.

The practice of your own dharma ensures that jnana arises, which enables true vairagya of the mind.

Aishvarya Bhava

It is only when you have sincerely practised dharma bhava, which has given rise to jnana and vairagya bhavas that there arises self-efficacy and self-reliance. Aishvarya bhava is reflected in the determination, strength, courage, self-confidence and power of the will of the individual, which arises from perceptive wisdom.

Aishvarya bhava brings forth humility and compassion as qualities that develop from a fullness of wisdom. It eradicates vanity and arrogance and makes the individual a strong and powerful being who rises above the ordinary. Aishvarya bhava manifests as assertiveness devoid of arrogance.

Aishvarya bhava is revealed in clarity of thought and purpose. It is attainment of physical, mental, moral finesse and spiritual fineness.

THE FOUR UNDESIRABLE BHAVAS

There are four undesirable bhavas.

Adharma

A misunderstanding of what your own true dharma is results in a false sense of satisfaction of the practice of dharma. For instance, if you are unwell and yet fast, under a notion of performing a religious act you are actually harming yourself. This brings on ill health and burdens the entire family. This is himsa or hurting yourself as well as the others around. This is adharma as looking after one's health is the primary dharma, duty of all beings.

Yoga discourages fasting but encourages partaking a moderate sattvika diet. It is here that you must understand the difference between Samkhya Yoga practice and religious rituals.

Adharma occurs when harm is caused to oneself through non-performance of one's duties towards personal, physical, mental and spiritual well-being. For example, you know you must practise asanas daily, but so often you neglect them. Or you give in to your emotions and tend to indulge in many things and lose self-control.

It is also manifested in personal grudges, likes and dislikes, hatred, envy, jealousy and greed.

Thus, adharma represents a lack of self-direction, self-commitment and self-motivation.

It results in stress, illness, chaos and confusions. Both the mind and the body become afflicted.

Ajnana

When, instead of wisdom, the arrogance of knowledge arises, such knowledge is mere information and not perspective astuteness. It destroys your character and makes you resort to pettiness. Ajnana also gives rise to several vices and mental disturbances.

There is lack of clarity which results in disorientation and confused states of mind. The individual is caught in a frenzy, resulting in a meltdown.

There is misunderstanding and misapprehension. It is the ignorance of not knowing the difference between the permanent and impermanent, pure and impure, painful and non-painful, real and unreal and the pure conscious self and materiality.

Raga

Raga or attachment is the greatest vice. It is a senseless clinging on to things, people and even one's thoughts. It inhibits growth of yourself as well as others' around. It is seen in parents' uncontrollable attachment to their children and overpowering their lives. It is visible between spouses who dominate and intimidate the other. Deep attachments in different relationships create irresolvable conflicts. Raga creates aversion when expectations are not met. For instance, when two close friends become attached to each other, expectations begin. When these expectations remain unfulfilled, aversion and anger build up.

Raga is also great attachment to material possessions despite the knowledge that you have to leave everything behind on the last passing moment and nothing is permanent.

Raga is that which stems from intense likes and dislikes. It creates the interplay of extreme love and hate. All pettiness and greed arise from raga. The mind becomes dull or agitated when situations go out of control.

Anaishvarya

When adharma, ajnana and raga dominate your mind and actions, there can be no peace.

There is fear, insecurity, lack of faith, low self-esteem resulting in depression. It is also characterized by self-dejection and hopelessness.

Or, it can result in the lack of humility and give rise to arrogance and overconfidence, which lead to ruin.

INTEGRATION OF THE CONCEPT OF
BHAVAS TO THE PRACTICE OF YOGA TECHNIQUES

The conglomerate of the eight bhavas forms the substratum of personal growth or downfall. The practice of dharma, jnana, vairagya and aishvarya lead to self-development and a positive transformation of your personality, whereas the opposite bhavas negate the beneficial effects leading to chaos.

The integrated practice of the four positive bhavas encompasses every action that you perform in life, irrespective of how insignificant or how great the action may be. Hence, apart from its influence in every aspect of life, at The Yoga Institute, its practice is interwoven in all yoga techniques to enable you to understand how they influence your entire mind–body–spirit schematics. Every practice has its corresponding effect within the physiology of the being. These effects relate to the four bhavas.

The presence of one bhava in a practice is always more pronounced than the others. Thus, it may be that one bhava is predominant while the other bhavas play a subsidiary role.

For example, meditative postures are categorized in the dharma bhava as its predominant bhava, yet, they do give rise to knowledge (jnana bhava). They create detachment from irrelevant thoughts (vairagya bhava) and sitting in that posture for a longer duration encourages self-discipline and strength (aishvarya bhava).

The effects of any practice of yoga, when practised in this manner, extend to the physical, emotional, ethical, spiritual and sensual faculties. Each practice has all these dimensions interwoven within to make it a complete practice.

The bhavas are also a part of pranayamas and kriyas. Jnana bhava is predominant in the practice of the pranayamas and aishvarya bhava is infused in the practice of the kriyas with the other bhavas playing subsidiary roles.

Since we recognize this relation and influence of the mind over body and body over mind, the application of the mental conditioning of the bhavas with any technique enhances the wholesomeness of the practice, its experience and effect.

When the bhavas are applied to the physical practices, the mind works in integration with the body to create a holistic and more intense effect rather than when a technique is practised in isolation, which could well make it any other form of exercise!

The mission of The Yoga Institute is to take the yoga seeker from and through the bahiranga (external) practices towards an inner journey, experiencing the antaranga (inner equanimity).

2

ASANA DEFINED

When people say they are going for a yoga class they generally mean an asana class. However, asana is a small part of yoga whereas yoga is the comprehensive whole, including the body–breath–mind–intellect–spirit complex.

In the yoga sutras of Maharishi Patanjali, asana is a part of the eight-fold path called Ashtanga Yoga. Ashtanga Yoga comprises of yamas which deal with an entire value system and niyamas which is related to personal disciplines. Ashtanga means eight limbs or branches, of which an asana or physical yoga posture is merely one branch, breath while or pranayama is another. These four stages form the bahiranga yoga sadhana.

A liaison between the outer and inner stages of personal growth is through pratyahara.

The last three inner stages are dharana, dhyana and samadhi. These three form the antaranga yoga sadhana (the inner journey of yoga). The sutras on antaranga yoga of Maharishi Patanjali are briefly explained in the section on meditative postures. This inward journey is expressed extensively throughout this book, especially through the inspiring thoughts and the philosophical introduction.

The explanation of asanas in the yoga sutras of Maharishi Patanjali has been limited to only three sutras. No explanations about names of asanas or their processes have been described in the sutras.

'Sthira sukham āsanam' II. 46
An asana is that which is (held) steady and is comfortable.

'Prayatna śaithilyam ananta samāpatibhyām' II. 47

10

The efforts of long practice create infinite absorption. (The mind becomes unshakable.)

'Tatah dvandva anābhighātah.' II. 48
Then, dualities no longer afflict.

ETYMOLOGY OF ASANA

An etymological explanation for the word 'asana' is found in the *Kamadhenu Tantra* where 'a' represents atmasiddhi (self-actualization), 'sa' stands for sarvarogapratibandha (prevention of all diseases) and 'na' represents siddhiprapti (gaining mastery).

OTHER DEFINITIONS

Asana is understood as that which is performed within a defined space. 'It is the manner of sitting or the seat whereon one sits' says Vachaspati Mishra, an early proponent of Samkhya Yoga.

In the traditional sense, asanas have no external aids. They involve using your body weight and a mat.

Asana is that which brings about steadiness of the mind and body. It regulates body rhythms and enables a deeper understanding of the entire body and its correlation with the breath and mind. Asanas are not to be taken as any form of exercise but as a comprehensive system of body–breath–mind management. The body strengthened by the fire of Hatha Vidya, the practice of the physical techniques described in the book, becomes a vehicle to spiritual ascent.

The Hatha Yoga Texts

The *Hatha Yoga Pradipika*, an ancient text on yoga, says one gains firmness and lightness of body, good health and a clear and balanced mind through practice. There is an awakening of dormant energy, purification of impurities, creation of balance and removal of pains.

Only fifteen asanas are described, especially those that are acknowledged by the great sages.

The text reveals that whether one is young, old, sick, weak or even normal, one can practise yoga. It further states that success in yoga is not achieved through reading scriptures alone, or by wearing a specific type of dress, or by talking about it. It is only through abhyasa (dedicated practice) that success in yoga can be achieved.

According to *Gheranda Samhita*, another early text on yoga practices, there is no force as powerful as yoga and its mastery leads to self-realization. There are thirty-two asanas explained.

The ancient text, *Shiva Samhita* mentions eighty-four asanas but only four are discussed.

All these texts culminate in a higher spiritual realm to be achieved as they clearly say that asanas, pranayamas, kriyas and other techniques prepare the body for spiritual realization.

ARE ASANAS THERAPEUTIC?

Traditionally the Hatha Yoga texts mention the physiological, therapeutic, psychological and spiritual benefits of asanas and other practices such as pranayamas, bandhas, mudras and kriyas, apart from meditative techniques. The aim of the practices was not to remove illnesses but their practice ensured good health and removal of problems.

Today too, there is a growing trend in using yoga practices to relieve oneself of illnesses and pains. It is valid insofar as you remember that once free from such obstacles yoga practices are for a much deeper and transcendental purpose.

Keeping in mind that the body is the most precious vehicle you have been blessed with, through which you can achieve whatever you wish, it becomes your fundamental duty to care for it, nourish it and keep it free from ailments so that your higher goals in life may be accomplished.

Often, people ask which specific practices will remove certain physical health problems. The techniques of yoga, it must be remembered, are not an instantaneous 'cure all'. Its practice must be for a long time along with its psychological and spiritual dimensions for a lasting effect. The new trends in yoga are mostly related to the physical level alone which reduces it to a form of exercise and fashion statements which greatly reduces its wholesomeness.

DIFFERENCE BETWEEN ASANAS AND OTHER FORMS OF EXERCISES

The purpose of yoga practices, especially asanas, is to create optimum health, body awareness and understanding at all levels, gross and subtle. Yoga practice reduces nervousness and weaknesses of the body and makes it fit to face adverse life situations.

Asanas are slow, deliberate, non-violent and non-competitive and performed with full concentration. During dynamic asana practice, the mind is continuously engaged in the activity and awareness is directed to the changes taking place in the sensations in various parts of the body.

During meditative asana practice, you may be required to hold the posture in its final position for a long time. This is to provide the opportunity to go beyond bodily experiences and engage in reflection and meditation.

Yoga practices have an anabolic effect. For example, after finishing an asana you may feel more energetic. They promote cell rejuvenation and energy production.

However, there is less calorie burning and hence no extra food or nutrition intake is necessary such as excess protein or protein shakes and similar products.

The practice of yoga makes a person calm, confident, self-assured, empathetic and self-aware.

The other physical practices that are mainly aimed at fitness; building stamina, endurance, muscle; and developing skills (sports, combat) are competitive. Generally the movements are repetitive, fast and sometimes violent. Mental engagement in the practice may not be there. For instance, in a gym you may continue to talk or watch TV and simultaneously continue the repetitive movement.

Gadgets and instruments are used in many types of other physical practices and methods.

There is a catabolic effect activity and hence most of the physical practices make a person tired. The effect of most of the physical systems is increased food intake and enhancement of appetite. Some practices may necessitate a particular kind of diet of animal protein, or fortified foods or extra vitamins and minerals.

Most importantly, other physical practices may not have such a marked influence on the personality and mind. Some systems may make you more competitive, intolerant and aggressive.

This book is not intended as a teachers' manual or students' handout but is for anyone who sincerely wishes to practise yoga in a wholesome manner.

3

BODY LANGUAGE

A dialogue with your body reveals hidden facets about yourself that you rarely realize. You need to love and care for yourself, not with a fanatic mindset which leads to obsessive disorders but with a genuine concern for personal growth at all levels. Your body has its own distinctive language of communication beyond the spoken word.

The senses give rise to bodily experiences which become known to you through certain signs. Hence, listen to the subtle signals—a pain here or there, discomforts, mood swings and so on. Among these, you need to distinguish between the real pain and the pleasurable pain of stretching an unused muscle. You need to understand your potential and know how to develop it. You need to be aware of your limitations as well.

A beginner in yoga needs to understand his personal health, age and capacity. For instance, a sixty- or a ninety-year-old may be extremely fit and flexible whereas a thirty-year-old may be inflexible.

This book recommends simple beginnings. The body has to be moulded gently and with patience. Yoga is not a competitive sport and each one of us is different, especially as householders, the approach must be of gradual progress.

The body, on commencing practice, will experience stretches, slight pulls and you will feel unused muscles being worked. After a session, you may feel pain in certain areas. Here you must be able to differentiate, as said before, between a pleasant pain of an unused muscle being stretched and pain that creates discomfort, like an injury. In the latter case, the pain may go away after a few days and in some cases a physician's advice and treatment may become pertinent.

Sometimes people complain of aches and pains after a yoga

session. They should take care not to overdo any practice, especially if one is a beginner. For instance, a lady always complained of backache after every intense asana practice session. Since this became a frequent phenomenon for her, listening to her body and refraining from overdoing the practices and trying to find out which of the practices was affecting her back became imperative.

Warming up the body thoroughly through pre-asana warm-ups as explained in the section on Sahaj Bhavasanas is essential.

The body acts in accordance with the mind, intellect and the breath. The dialogue between the body and the self becomes fruitful when each is in harmony with the other.

4

CONCENTRATION OF THE MIND AND BALANCE OF THE BODY

Balance is the outcome of neuromuscular coordination and mental concentration. Both concentration and balance are interrelated. For example, if you try to practise Talasana with your eyes closed you are bound to lose your balance. Thus, in every posture it is important to know how and where to concentrate.

Balancing is an art that comes with practice. Its medium is concentration. Concentration is attention to one and inattention to everything else. Such concentration prevents yoga from becoming a mechanical practice and makes it a transformative and spiritual experience.

There is a story in the Upanishads of a dancer dancing with a pot on her head. She moves gracefully and rhythmically through all the steps, but her awareness is always on the pot on her head. This story teaches us three things. First, though the body moves in different ways the attention and awareness is vital in maintaining balance without either the object of concentration getting disturbed or the body movements going awry. Second, though the concentration is on the object, the grace and perfection of the body movements do not get disturbed. Third, it is the story of life; despite all its movements in different and difficult directions, a firm faith in the higher existence remains a constant focus.

In the context of asana practice or any other yoga practice it is vital to be fully involved in the practice and hence, in traditional yoga, there was no music played during yoga practice. Chanting, music and other such methods have their own place and not mixed with asanas. During the practice of yoga there must be absolute concentration to the practice and all its aspects of breathing, inculcating the bhava and the efforts towards reaching the final posture.

Thus, concentration and the resulting balance brings into effect steadiness of posture and the mind. This is how yoga has a wholesome effect on the entire persona of the being.

5

POSTURAL AWARENESS AND PRECISION

FUNCTION OF FORM

Form is the important substratum of most of the objects that manifest in the universe. It is within this form of a thing that countless activities and transformations take place. Sometimes as the form changes so does its function and again we see that a function may give rise to forms. This form is seen in nature, in living and non-living organisms, however microscopic they may be.

Form is also that which can be in the shape of ideation. It is said that for any creation, an idea 'forms' in the mind before manifestation.

In yoga, these multitudinous forms were used as inspirations to derive their respective benefits when replicated in the different asanas devised by the sages. It is said that there can be as many asanas as the number of species.

The asanas are modelled after nature, birds, animals, auspicious symbols, gurus and the human body. For instance, Talasana is an inspiration from the palm tree, Padmasana is based on the lotus flower and Ardha Matsyendrasana named after the great guru, Matsyendranatha. The objective of such inspirations for the postures is to create the corresponding qualities within you. For example, it is natural for the palm tree to rise upwards, grow and remain unshaken even in the strongest winds, or for the lotus to repel the murky water and mud around it and bloom despite its surroundings.

Each asana has a form that is formed when you arrive at the final position of the asana. Each form has its unique function such that it becomes the aim of that particular asana. Thus, the final pose depicts the characteristic of the name given to it.

FORM AND THE POSTURES

Indian philosophy encompasses the philosophy of rasa. It is the entire spectrum of human emotions that form a narrative of life. Within this scheme is included alankara or rasa shastra, the theory of aesthetics.

Each form has its exquisite charm and beauty that is seen outside and experienced within. The human form is beautiful and so is the mind, and it needs to be kept so. The practice of asanas must be graceful, rhythmic, mindful, creative and dynamic.

FORM AND THE MEDITATIVE POSTURES

Form is especially relevant in the meditative postures, which are mostly in the sitting position. When you sit forming a stable base, the legs are placed such that they allow the upper body to remain comfortably erect. The flow of prana decreases in the lower extremities (you may feel your feet going numb), and this flow is directed upwards towards the head region.

Yogendraji had mentioned such forms in his writings where emphasis was given, for example, to the triangle formation in meditative postures. For instance, an equilateral triangle is formed when sitting in Siddhasana. In Swastikasana, the auspicious symbol of a swastika is recreated, which denotes 'to be well, it is well and let it be well'. Formations of asanas are representative of such auspicious symbols. Forms, as symbols of divinity, are used for meditation and concentration.

Form and its function reproduce an aura of harmony, rhythm and also provide aesthetic values of grace and attractiveness.

Sri Aurobindo has said, 'Form is the rhythm of the Spirit.'

POSTURAL AWARENESS

Postural awareness is evident when we become aware of how we 'get into' the posture, remain in it and how we return to the starting position. Awareness at all these levels ensures a smooth and graceful movement. It is for this reason that the practices have been presented with the starting position, steps and posture release.

Remaining static in any posture there must be complete mind–body awareness. For example, in a sideward bending asana like Konasana there must be absolute awareness that the upper body does not tilt forwards while bending sidewards. Similarly, there must be awareness of the balance of the body, the toes, hands and so on when remaining in Talasana for a minute. Even a dynamic movement in Talasana is an effort for complete coordination.

PRECISION

Precision is achieved through regular and dedicated practice and you will be able to reach the final pose effortlessly.

Precision is measured in the efforts you put in to create awareness and concentration. It is in the ability to reach the final posture with ease and the gradual increase of the capacity to maintain the static poses. Thus, try not to be in a hurry to reach perfectness. Let it be a gradual but regular progression.

According to Maharishi Patanjali, the efforts (yatna) that you must put into the practice (abhyasa) are dirgha kala (for a long time), nairantarya (without a break), satkarya (with absolute dedication) and asevito (regularly and systematically). This kind of devoted practice will create a dradha bhumi (a firm and strong foundation) for all-round growth and progress.

6

DYNAMICS OF MOVEMENT

Movement is an intrinsic part of life. The way any movement occurs reflects its cause and effect arrangement. Movement is time.

The way in which a person moves, speaks and carries himself is known as body language. The body speaks through its different movements. Even the process of breathing is about motion.

In yoga, it is the subtlest movement of the thoughts that need to be monitored, prevented and mastered as the very nature of thoughts is about their constant motion.

The movement from the gross to subtle awareness needs to arise. The body is the gross medium of the abode of consciousness. It enshrines different facets of thought, breath and other faculties. As the body moves so do the senses, breath and thoughts and vice versa.

While performing the asanas, the movements are slow, steady, gradual, graceful and rhythmic. The breath is synchronized with all movements. When an asana is performed with body–breath–thought harmonized movement, the effects are experienced as a transformation of the entire personality. Thus, slow movements are invaluable rather than fast-paced movements, especially when performing asanas as when performing any asana quickly there remains no time for coordination or any spiritual reflection. For instance, the current trend of performing a hundred Surya Namaskaras mechanically and quickly is not a traditional idea. Performed even once in the morning, facing the east, with utmost care, concentration, perfection of each posture, chanting of the mantras and with total reverence is an experience.

Movement and steadiness form two sides of the same coin, opposite to each other but vital in the progress of life.

DYNAMIC VERSUS STATIC MODES

The cultural postures can be practised in the dynamic or static modes.

Dynamic Mode

The dynamic mode of the postures ensures the entire body is in a state of flow. The various movements involving the different joints in the body are meant to keep it supple. The aim of the postures is to increase flexibility. Controlled, smooth and graceful movement enables the muscles to stretch, expand, contract and relax. Such movements will help avoid injuries and result in a lean and flexible body.

Static Mode

The static mode of the postures works on the isometric group of muscles. Holding a position helps with building the overall strength, endurance and core stability. In the static condition, the entire body undergoes changes at the cellular level. The modification of a muscle and/or muscle group takes place. A greater level of skill and endurance capacity is needed to hold a posture. You will learn to enjoy the moments of pause, feel the contractions and stretches of muscles.

However, caution must be taken when the body is held in a static state for more than a minute or two. Returning back to a normal position must be slow. The longer you hold the posture, returning to the normal position must also be slow as the muscles must be released gradually. If you come to the normal position too quickly the stretched muscle may tend to snap causing an injury or certain areas may go numb. Static positions require long practice. The time recommended in static positions is from a few seconds to one or two minutes. More than that is not required for the full benefit of an asana to occur.

Unless it is a meditative posture, it is not recommended to stay too long in any posture.

Both formats of dynamic and static postures make for leaner, flexible and stronger muscles over a period of time. The joints remain flexible, there is an increase in bone density and mass, healthy organs and the overall result is good vitality and health of mind and body. Of course, the true purpose of asanas is spiritual ascent, as asanas and other yoga practices are techniques to make the body strong for further intense asanas, and other practices are not an end in themselves.

Such physical benefits may occur with any form of exercise, but a complete and wholesome experience arises when any yoga technique is practised with the mind–body–breath synchronization.

7

THE YOGA WAY OF EATING

In all kinds of physical training, the 'core' of the body is emphasized, as it forms the central space from which the entire energy creation and distribution begins. The abdominal cavity is the region in which the important organs of the body are housed. The assimilation, digestion and distribution of nutrients from food, the filtration system have effects on all the other systems.

THE VITAL ROLE OF FOOD

Whatever you do in life, each activity that you perform, whether through body, speech or thought is all founded on the substratum of food, say the Upanishads.

The *Taittiriya Upanishad* says, food is '*annam brahmeti*' (food is Brahman, the highest reality and conscious principle). It adds, '*Annam na nindayat tad vratam*' (do not criticize food, that is the pledge), '*na parichakshita tad vratam*' (do not despise food, that is the pledge). You are born from food, subsist because of it and pass away into food (matter).

Ayurveda, the science of life and health, explains the different kinds of food for healthy living. However, the aims of Ayurveda and yoga are little different. Ayurveda is about health, freedom from diseases and longevity. Yoga upholds the spiritual ascent as highest in all its endeavours. Thus in yoga, all kinds of meat are prohibited as they are acquired by killing a living creature and killing is himsa (violence) and against the fundamental yoga principle of ahimsa (non-violence).

Sattvika foods, such as fresh seasonal fruits and vegetables, whole

25

local grains, cereals (not boxed and processed), lentils, pulses should form the staples. Locally available grains, such as rice, millets and whole wheat are ideal sources of complex carbohydrates and energy.

Cow's milk and its products are recommended in yoga especially pure ghee. Those who want to avoid milk and its products must ensure that the levels of vitamin B12 are maintained.

Dried fruits such as dates (highly recommended in yoga texts), figs, raisins and others can be eaten daily along with nuts, especially walnuts and almonds in small quantities. Whole peanuts and other such locally cultivated nuts also can be had. Instead of refined sugar, you can opt for natural unrefined sugars such as gud (jaggery), raw sugar, molasses or leaves of stevia. Honey can be had only if you are sure of its source being natural and unrefined, but in small quantities.

Spices such as turmeric, coriander, cumin, ajwain (caraway seeds), cloves, cinnamon, cardamom, pepper and other such spices are essential in small measures.

Salt is to be had but in small amounts. The preferred salt is natural sea salt or mineral/rock (black/red, pink or white) salts. Sea salt can be added during cooking whereas mineral salts are best sprinkled on top.

Onions and garlic have medicinal properties and are considered as rajasika foods.

Fats that are recommended in yoga are pure ghee, unrefined and cold pressed oils such as sesame, mustard, peanut, coconut or any other which is locally available. The best oils are seed and nut oils and not from vegetable sources.

You must eat more of the local fresh produce than expensive imported items. For instance, there is a craze in India for eating quinoa, which is quite expensive. Do not forget that the humble rajagra (amaranth) eaten during fortnightly fasts is an excellent substitute. Or, the red quinoa sold in fancy store isles in western countries is quite the same as the Indian ragi (nachani). Each food culture arises from its local produce over generations and proves to be most healthy over time.

The Hatha Yoga texts explain how, when and what is to be

eaten. Fasting (nirahara) and even eating once a day (ekahara) is not recommended in yoga if you have followed mitahara (moderation in food).

Four meals a day are ideal. You can also divide your meals into two main meals and two smaller meals according to your lifestyle. However, there are some people who eat only once, twice or thrice a day do very well. Eating too often is undesirable in yoga.

It helps to have a nutritious breakfast which will sustain you till lunch. Lunch should be light or according to your work schedules. An evening light snack can be followed by a simple dinner which keeps you satiated but not so heavy that it disturbs your sleep.

In the yoga texts, the stomach is roughly divided into four sections; two sections must be filled with food, one section with liquid, such as thin buttermilk, diluted lime water, soup, thin lentil soup, but not water. The remaining section must be left free. Remember that each one has a different stomach capacity and different requirements. Hence, no fixed amount or calories are specified.

Yoga helps you to understand the spiritual dimension of food and its corresponding role in the growth of a spiritual being. It helps to elevate you from the mere physical to the aware and conscious state. You must understand that food is that which sustains you, helps you grow as well as enables you to develop a relationship with the Divine. Food that you eat must be Shiva samprityam (that which can be offered to and pleasing to God).

Food and eating is a yajna, a spiritual offering into the jatharagni, the stomach, which is of the nature of the sacred fire.

8

BUILDING PHYSICAL AND PSYCHOLOGICAL STRENGTH AND SPIRITUAL AWARENESS

Through the practice of yoga, with complete understanding, there arises physical strength which is not about being able to lift weights, run marathons or build six-pack abs, but it is about fitness that makes you endure life's daily problems with grace. In Indian philosophy, it is called svasthya, complete all-round health and freedom from diseases. The body is able to withstand the dualities of life and reduce the impact of ageing.

Accompanied by a holistic practice as described, it transforms the way in which you respond to people and situations around. It makes you understand both the strengths and frailties of human nature making you more perceptive, adaptable and giving you the inner power to remain quite unaffected by the vagaries of the world and life.

Yogendraji had said that yoga is a part of life, practised every moment. The asanas, pranayamas and other techniques may be performed for some time in the day, but true yoga is the absolute management of the mind resulting in self-mastery.

To realize the immense value of a holistic yoga practice, you must rise beyond the mere physical. A healthy body becomes a vehicle; a temple for mental and spiritual growth.

Hence arises a spiritual awakening; the dawn of a new and transformed 'you'.

9

THE QUESTION OF PERFECTION

Often, you hear people talking of perfection. Is it possible to attain it?

In yoga, people say you must attain the perfect posture. Seeing models effortlessly perform several yoga postures makes you wonder whether you can perform them. For instance, you may reach a stage where you perform every posture perfectly and effortlessly, then what? Then, boredom and stagnation arises, as the mind will always want something more. Hence, true yoga is beyond the scope of physical perfection.

That is why there is the eternal question of perfection. No human being is perfect. If you are perfect then you are not human. We are all on a journey. We are all seekers. Each of us is different, having individual capacities, potentialities and unique qualities. At The Yoga Institute, all seekers are called sadhakas. They are given a wide scope of progressing in their own unique ways.

On this path, you are recommended to follow according to your own capacities and abilities. You must ensure your targets and goals that you set for yourself are high enough but not so high that you may give up easily. Perfection is about self-discipline.

Perfection is not a general phenomenon but a special one. Each one of you is seeking your own perfection. It is incomparable. Hence, in yoga there is no competition, as it is not based on physical excellence alone but on each individual's growth on all levels of existence and potentials.

Perfection is about developing the potential that you possess, which will facilitate a physical experience to be translated into psychological and spiritual equipoise.

10

YOGA FOR ALL

Yoga has become the new-age health and fitness fad. If we were to google 'yoga', immediately images of slim young women and men appear. We would wonder where the ordinary human being, struggling to keep up with the pressures of daily life, fits in. To address the issue we have chosen Samartha and Pramila, who are not professional models but trained teachers of The Yoga Institute, to demonstrate the asanas for this book. Pramila is the mother of three young children, who practises yoga regularly, in body, mind and spirit.

Going to any yoga class could be quite intimidating for many as fit people easily turn and twist their bodies, which can leave many folks in dismay, as their fitness and flexibility levels do not match up!

In this book, we have tried to bust certain myths about who can practise yoga. First, yoga is mind management. It is keeping the mind balanced and trying our best to remain unaffected by the ups and downs of life. The philosophical principles must go hand in hand with any physical practice; otherwise any physical practice will be reduced to mere exercise. Second, all practices, including asanas, pranayama and other techniques must be practised with concentration and right approach of the mind and the intellect. In this book, all the practices have been modified and simplified by the gurus of The Yoga Institute to suit the modern person with a busy life.

Thus, all practices explained in this book have variations from simple to the difficult. Hansaji's Sahaj Bhavasanas are vital as they include a wide range of practices that can be done standing, sitting and lying down.

In describing the suitability of practices for different people, two separate terms 'yoga' and 'asanas' are used, the reason being to distinguish between yoga, which is an all-encompassing term to include the mind and intellect and asanas, which refer to the body.

This book is not aimed as therapy and hence the instructions for the practices are general. Illnesses of different natures require specific guidance from doctors as well as trained yoga therapists. The limitations and contraindications serve as a general guide.

YOGA AND ASANAS FOR CHILDREN

Children have flexible bodies and become experts at asanas quickly. They can be taught meditative and relaxation practices for short durations as 5 to 10 minutes to calm their restlessness. The age when they can begin practice ranges from 6 to 7 years when they have some understanding. Some postures are excellent for developing concentration.

It must be ensured that asanas do not become just a physical drill; their sanctity is maintained by teaching them life values too. Children need a different way of being taught as pranayamas are not recommended for young children and neither is the Yogendra breathing rhythm or counts. They should not hold their breath.

YOGA AND ASANAS FOR THE YOUNG

Pre-adolescents and adolescents have their own unique requirements. Puberty entails growth in all areas from biological, psychological to intellectual which need discipline. The cultural asanas can be practised by them both in dynamic and static modes. Meditative practices along with the unique practices of The Yoga Institute are especially helpful in understanding their personal goals and abilities. Pranayamas and kriyas enable them to achieve good health and clarity of thought.

YOGA AND ASANAS FOR WOMEN

Women have distinctive biological and psychological needs. They are emotionally strong yet sensitive.

It is advisable for them to avoid yoga practices during periods, especially during the heavy-flow days. However, regular practice helps in reducing pre-menstrual syndrome and bloating and also helps to relieve menstrual cramps. Practices during pregnancy are best under the guidance of a trained teacher.

A holistic yoga practice ensures a healthy and supple body. In yoga, the aim is not to become wafer-thin but to remain healthy. A balance of weight occurs through regular practice. All practices in this book are excellent for women but care must be taken according to age and other health conditions.

YOGA FOR HOMEMAKERS AND WORKING PEOPLE

Modern life is very busy leaving little time for daily asanas and other yoga practices. Hansaji believes that for daily practice you must become very aware and mindful at all times and in all activities. She has the following guidelines for working people, whether at home, office or outside.

1. When you wake up in the morning, avoid getting up from the bed immediately. For a few moments reflect on the quality of your sleep quality without delving into its analysis, stretch out in Yashtikasana. Follow it up with bending each knee as in Pavanamuktasana. Bend one leg at a time and place the foot on the opposite thigh or cross the legs while still lying in bed.
    Sit up turning to one side. Cross your legs and watch your breath for a minute. This entire process takes only five minutes but it readies you for the day.
2. After brushing your teeth, practise Jivha Mula Shodhana. This will induce a clear bowel movement. You can drink a glass of hot or warm water before this practice.
3. Bathing must be mindful. Besides cleansing your body, it removes dead skin, invigorates your body and eases all your stress and tension accumulated in the muscles and tissues.

Make this into a prayer. Stand under the shower in a pose of prayer and allow the water to soak your body for a few seconds. Keep your eyes open as you do not want to lose balance. Soap yourself and as you do so, bend and scrub your legs and feet, touching your feet as in Hastapadasana. Once soaping is over, rub your body as the water rinses the soap off. During this process, bend sidewards, forward and finally look up and allow the water to run down your throat. Also ensure that the bathroom is well-ventilated.

This entire process should not take more than five minutes. Dry yourself and wrap yourself in a loose robe.

Do not dress immediately. Sit in a comfortable meditative posture or lie down in Shavasana for a few minutes as it enables you to relax, and allows your body to get in tune with the external environment. This part is extremely important for an office-goer. In ancient times, worship or meditation was done after a bath. Today, we have entirely skipped this part. The idea here is about a mental conditioning as well as physical conditioning. During a bath, the body is relaxed, the muscles and tissues are not ready for the morning rush. Often we hear about heart attacks occurring in the morning after a shower. This process is a buffer to prepare the mind and the body for an active day.

4. During the entire day, try and keep a calm mind, approaching every event and situation with patience, grace and mindfulness of the self and others.

5. Before retiring for the night, practise reflection. Reflect upon the activities of the day without becoming too judgmental. Sit on a bed, and practise breathing alternately through your nostrils. This is not the practice of Yogendra Anuloma Viloma but a process of continuous breathing through alternate nostrils beginning with inhaling through your left nostril till you feel sleepy. This should take around 5 to 10 minutes. Sleep with a positive thought in mind so that it is sattvika and restful and you awake fresh.

YOGA FOR THE ELDERLY

Age is in the mind! Today there are ninety-plus people who are healthy and practise yoga and there are people in their thirties who are unable to practise.

However, the body does age biologically and certain things must be kept in mind such as, always to remain within limits and never overdo any practice, as in case of any injury, healing as one grows old is a long process. Hansaji's Sahaj Bhavasanas are extremely useful for the elderly or the sick.

This book has several variations, especially in the section of Sahaj Bhavasanas, for those who cannot stand or sit. However, it is important to remember this book is a general book and not aimed as therapy. Thus, in case of any medical problems, guidance from an expert, a doctor or a trained yoga professional is of utmost value.

Keeping in mind these guidelines of who can practise yoga and asanas, you can begin your practice.

11

THE YOGA ASANA PRACTICE

BEGINNING WITH A PLAN

Setting a goal by writing down a plan is the first step. It helps in both clarity of thought and action. To set a goal is to do something at will. This is the beginning of yoga. It is to take charge of your mind, intellect and body. This responsibility and actions therefrom will ensure appropriate results. However, here the aim is not seeking results immediately but concentrating on the effective practice. The results will spontaneously occur.

TIME

Such a plan will have to fit in comfortably with your daily schedules. At the outset, you may decide to allocate at least 30 to 40 minutes of undisturbed time daily for yoga practices considering it as a duty to yourself.

The best time for yoga practice is before breakfast. But, let it not be a pretext to miss a session on certain occasions. Thus, choose anytime during the day that suits you. Later you can increase the duration to about an hour.

An important idea in yoga is to see that the calm created during the practice session is extended throughout the day and infuses every activity.

Of course, there will be some days when you may not have the time or are unwell. Do not fret or feel guilty as accepting situations and circumstances is also yoga. However, this should not be an excuse not to practise.

On such days, practise for a shorter duration or modify the time but remember it is your personal commitment. During such occasions, you can choose one or two asanas from each section (standing, sitting and supine) and perform just one or two repetitions so that in a short time span you are putting your body through all movements. Take care to warm up properly through the specified Sahaj Bhavasanas.

Please maintain a record of your practice schedule. Of course you can be flexible as rigidity causes more problems. A record will help in future reflections.

OTHER SUGGESTIONS

It is best to practise asanas when you have clean bowels. You may drink a glass or two of slightly warm water before commencing asanas. Breathable and comfortable clothes are ideal yoga wear.

The physical practices are not recommended on a full stomach. So leave aside a couple of hours after a heavy meal.

DYNAMIC VS STATIC POSTURES

Please refer to Chapter 6, Dynamics of Movement, to decide whether you want to choose the dynamic version or maintain the posture in a static form for no more than two minutes in relation to the cultural postures.

THE PLACE

Once you have decided on the time of practice, at home, choose a well-ventilated room, not too sunny and not too dark. Always try to use your own personal mat. If the temperature is too hot or cold adjust it according to your comfort.

It is best not to have too many people going in or out of the room. This is your personal space and time. However, if this is impossible see that you do not get distracted by the diversions and remain quiet.

In case of any disturbances, let them not affect you but continue your practice after attending to them. For instance, if you have to attend to an important phone call or answer the doorbell, it is best to attend to that with a calm mind and resume your practice once you have finished with the task.

In case you wish to practise some of the asanas in office or somewhere else, adjust your plan accordingly keeping in mind the possible distractions.

If you are practising in a common area such as a park, gym, studio or yoga class, maintain an internal awareness and focus on yourself rather than getting distracted by anything or anyone else.

While travelling you can try to carry a small folding mat with you as it carries your vibrations generated through your yoga practice.

When the space is settled, choose a series of practices from this book. Try to follow a pattern without being too strict about the sequence of asanas. Again this series can be changed from time to time. This will avoid monotony as well as bring in vairagya bhava as we remain unattached even to a particular format.

THE YOGA MAT

Today an entire industry has arisen, selling yoga merchandise. Keep a few basics in mind while purchasing a yoga mat, such as check whether it is anti-skid and washable or easily cleanable. It would be beneficial if the mat is made from natural fibres rather than synthetic material.

PLANNING YOUR YOGA ASANA SESSION

Plan your yoga session with all seriousness as it will bring out the best from within you. It will result in freedom from chronic problems, good sleep, lightness, a spring in the step and many more physiological benefits. But above all, a peaceful and calm mind, will make you more self-confident.

Begin with Conditioning. In Sukhasana, sit comfortably watching your breath to bring the mind to a focused state and away from external disturbances. This may take anywhere between 5 to 15 minutes depending on the time you have or how soon you can steady your mind. Refrain from sitting too long if the mind is disturbed. This is not a meditation session but to 'gather' the outgoing mind and bring it inwards to concentrate on yoga practices.

SEQUENCE OF PRACTICE

1. Commence with conditioning and selected Sahaj Bhavasanas to warm up the body.
2. Follow them with standing postures, then sitting postures followed by supine postures and conclude with Shavasana.
3. Once rested, practise your selected pranayamas.
4. Take a pause (anywhere from a few seconds to a minute, depending on your physical fitness and mental state) in-between each asana as it will enable you to reflect on the bhava of the next posture, its connectedness to the previous one and brings in unity to the entire session. This will also enable you to remember the purpose of asana practice, which is for emotional and spiritual growth; its physical benefits being by-products.

BEGINNER'S LEVEL

If you are a beginner, it is best to devise a weekly or monthly plan and write it down.

This plan can include a regime of physical practices, time for conditioning or simple meditation along with a food plan. Such a plan entails you put in efforts to maintain a balanced mind-state to experience a totality of experience.

When you are new to any practice, it must be kept in mind that initially it may not be possible for a harmonious and seamless practice, integrating the movement, the breath and the concentration, especially when a teacher is physically unavailable and you are following instructions from the book. Hence, you can begin with a trial of the movement only for a couple of rounds. This can be followed with integrating the breathing patterns and once you are comfortable, introduce the bhava into the mind while holding the position for the specified duration.

Another idea is to record the instructions in your own voice and listen to them as you practise, so you do not have to refer to the book at every stage.

As you continue your practise regularly you will find that you slowly remember the breathing rhythm and are able to focus on the bhava too.

The beginner is also cautioned not to expect miraculous results.

It is advised to be in tune with the changes within your body. In case you feel tired in-between an asana it is recommended you practise Nishpanda Bhava (an institutional practice) or even Trataka, a kriya for the eyes (it is a practice to enhance concentration).

INTERMEDIATE LEVEL

The same process can be followed as before except now that you have become familiar with the different practices and can easily manage the postural movements and breath coordination, you can practise more repetitions.

You can introduce the next level of complex asanas. Staying static in some postures is also recommended.

ADVANCED LEVEL

The advanced practitioner can change sequences and practise more repetitions. However, the best experiences can be derived when remaining static in a posture. It brings about complete mind–body–breath awareness.

12

DIFFERENT TYPES OF ASANAS

MEDITATIVE ASANAS

When all the indriyas (senses) are at rest, the I -ness'
withdraws itself, allowing buddhi (the intellect) to experience
a state of equipoise.

A meditative posture induces a meditative state. It is not about how long you can remain in the posture but about its effects of serenity and quietude that are generated during that period which are extended throughout the day and infused in every activity.

It is restructuring the mind waves to a state of calm. Such is a meditative state, of repose and equipoise.

Patanjali's *Yoga Sutras* on dharana and dhyana:

'Deśa bandhasya cittasya dhāranā' III. 1
Dharana is when the mind stuff is held concentrated in one place.

'Tatra pratyaya eka tānatā dhyānam' III. 2
Then (when the mind force) is held onto that one essence/place for an extended/continuous duration is dhyana.

A meditative practice leads to a state of quietude. There is mindfulness and a realization of being in the present. Meditation is the asana for the mind.

A NOTE FOR ALL MEDITATIVE PRACTICES

1. Once you are comfortably settled in the posture close your eyes, relax your facial muscles and passively observe your breath.
2. If you are a beginner, it may take some time to get adjusted and comfortable in the posture. Begin with a short duration and extend the time as you become proficient in the practice.

   The mind may wander but gently keep bringing it back to focus on your breath or the chosen object of concentration.
3. In case the mind gets distracted, you may choose to focus on an external object such as a steady candle flame or a fixed point which may be an auspicious symbol.

   You may also choose to focus on an internal point such as the space between your eyebrows, your heart region or wherever you can remain focused for the duration you remain in the posture.
4. Practise for about 10 to 20 minutes daily extending the duration according to your time, schedule, requirement and desirability. For normal and active persons, including householders, sitting for too long, such as an hour or more is unnecessary, as it is the calm generated during the moderate amount of time of practice that has to be infused in all activities through the day.
5. It is best to open your eyes slowly to come out of any meditative state. You can also palm or cup your eyes for a few seconds and gently stretch the legs forward as you make gentle movements in the different parts of the body. In case the toes go numb, wriggle them and or rub them with your hands till the numbness wears off and then get up.

LIMITATIONS/CONTRAINDICATIONS
FOR ALL MEDITATIVE POSTURES

1. Acute arthritis: People suffering from moderate arthritis can modify the posture and practise sitting comfortably erect on a straight-backed chair without arms and maybe with one leg gently folded and tucked under the opposite thigh (if possible).

When sitting on a chair with your feet resting on the floor, keep a mat below your feet.

2. Depression: If you are feeling low or depressed it is recommended that you practise active or dynamic meditation where the posture remains the same but the attention is on any external object such as a steady flame of a candle, a flower, or any such object. You can also try counting backwards. This may be done for shorter durations to practise attentiveness and being distracted.

Conditioning*

Mindfulness is my fundamental duty.

Yogendraji had realized that it was not easy for a lay mind to quickly focus on a new or different activity. It needed a gathering of thoughts. Such a practice is called Conditioning.

At The Yoga Institute, the meditative posture, Sukhasana, is the instrumental practice to condition the mind. It is generally experienced that a state of meditation is not easily acquired, especially in a short duration of time. This led to the understanding that we must condition our minds prior to any practice. Conditioning is to withdraw the chattering and distract the mind inwards. It also helps in restructuring the mind.

This practice readies the mind for further practice of asanas, pranayamas and kriyas. It can also be practised independently to calm and steady the mind.

Conditioning can be practised by everyone. Even if you cannot sit in the meditative posture described, you can sit comfortably on a chair.

Method of Practice

1. Preferably sit in Sukhasana or on a straight-backed chair. Avoid practising on a sofa or on a bed. If you are on a chair and are able to bend your knees you can fold one leg and let the other leg down.
2. Take care to keep the back erect, the abdomen held in its normal contour. Check that you are not slouching. Keep your

head straight, elbows and shoulders relaxed, palms facing down, resting on the thighs or knees. There is no requirement of any hasta mudra or hand gestures.

3. Watch your breath for about 10 to 15 minutes. Try not to let the mind wander. However, in case it does, bring it back to watching the breath without getting disturbed.

Limitations / Contraindications

No limitations. This technique can be practised by all except as mentioned earlier.

Benefits

1. Conditioning greatly aids in bringing a distracted mind to attentiveness and aids concentration.
2. It reduces extraneous thoughts and makes you mindful, encouraging being in the present.
3. It brings clarity of thought and an inner harmony arises as there is less nervous agitation.

Meditative asanas begin with Conditioning followed by Sukhasana.

Sukhasana—The Easy or Pleasant Posture*

*I relish the feeling of peace and quietude, ensuring it extends
to all activities through the day.*

Sukhasana, as its name suggests is a simple posture that can be maintained easily for a long time. It enables one to steady the mind and body.

Sukhasana is the simplest technique to observe the life force. The spiritual dimension is embodied in the term 'sukha', where 'kha' represents the wisdom of being in tune with the spiritual and divine forces.

Method of Practice

Starting Position
1. Sit on a mat spread on the floor with legs fully stretched out and without taking the support of any wall or fixture.

Steps
2. Sit cross-legged and try to keep both knees equidistant up from the floor.
3. Gently place your hands on your respective thighs near the knees, palms facing downwards. There is no need for any hasta mudra.
4. Keep your body erect, abdomen in normal contour, head poised, chin parallel to the ground taking care not to stiffen your body.

The elbows should be aligned with your body such that they are not pushed outwards or pressed inwards but in a comfortable position.

5. Keep your shoulders relaxed, not drooping.
6. Sit in this position and watch your breath (or focus on any object of your choice).

Posture Release

7. Straighten both your legs as in the starting position.

Limitations / Contraindications

1. Acute arthritis.
2. Psychological disorder/depression.
3. As such there are no major limitations and can be safely practised by all with minor modifications like sitting on a chair with one leg folded.

Benefits

Physical

1. There is a correction of your posture.
2. It stretches your thighs, calves, ankles and hips.

Therapeutic

1. It improves flexibility of your lower extremities, especially the hip and knee joints.

Psychological

1. You are more aware of your body and breathing.
2. Your mind remains focused and your concentration improves.

3. This practice will make you mindful and encourage you to be in the present.
4. An inner harmony arises in you, as there is less nervous agitation.

Muscles Involved
1. Flexors and extensors of the vertebral column
2. Abductors, flexors and medial rotators of the hip
3. Knee and shoulder joint flexors

Padmasana—The Lotus Posture***

I blossom like the lotus flower,
remaining unaffected by the world around.

Padmasana is a traditional posture. The word 'padma' means a lotus. The manner in which the lotus grows amidst muddy water and yet blooms in full glory, remaining unaffected by its surroundings is brought to fruition in this asana. It is also a symbol of peace and highly favoured by the yogis.

Padmasana is reflective of the struggles of life which you can tide over to become stronger. It helps you to realize that you cannot change anyone but yourself.

This posture is not easy to achieve and maintain by everyone. But perseverance brings results. The formation of the body as the lotus will bring out its respective qualities within you. It ushers physical stability and psychological equanimity.

Method of Practice

Starting Position
1. Sit on a mat spread on the floor with your legs fully stretched out without taking support of any wall or fixture.

Steps
2. Commence by gently bending your right leg inwards at the knee joint, then fold it and with the aid of the hands place the right heel on the top of the left thigh in such a way that the right foot is placed with its sole turned upwards.

3.   Likewise, place your left heel with upturned soles over the right thigh so that the ankles cross each other. Preferably your heel ends should touch closely.
4.   Keep both your knees pressed to the ground as far as possible.
5.   Hold your body comfortably erect keeping your head, neck and trunk in a straight line. It is desirable to keep your abdomen moderately contoured inwards.
6.   Place your left hand just below the navel with your palm facing upwards. Place your right hand over the left hand with your palm facing upwards. Keep your shoulders and hands relaxed.
7.   Sit in this position, watching your breath or focus on any object of your choice.

Note: Alternate use of legs is recommended. Start with one minute and with regular practice take it up to 10 to 15 minutes or as per your comfort.

Posture Release
8.   Relax your hands to place them on your knees or thighs.
9.   With the help of your hands slowly lift your top leg and place it down and relax your other leg.
10. Straighten both your legs slowly as in the starting position.

Limitations / Contraindications
1.   Severe arthritis and/or stiffness of the lower limbs.
2.   Acute knee pain.
3.   Same as Sukhasana.

Benefits

Physical
1. It provides a good stretch to the thighs, calves, ankles and hips.
2. It corrects spinal irregularities.
3. It benefits the pelvic and lower abdomen region.

Therapeutic
1. There is a correction of your posture as the spine is held erect.
2. Flexibility of your lower extremities occurs and there is a stretch experienced in your ankle and knee joints.
3. Blood circulation in your abdominal area increases.
4. It helps to deal with your menstrual and sciatica issues.

Psychological
1. There is greater awareness of your body and your breathing.
2. It improves concentration as your mind remains attentive.

Muscles Involved
1. Hip abductors, flexors and medial rotators
2. Knees, elbows and ankle plantar flexors

Sthitaprarthanasana—The Standing Prayer Posture*

*Steadiness of my body is interrelated to
the steadiness of my breath and mind.*

A proper bearing of your body is essential for its physiological and psychological health.

Faulty postural habits cause slouching and sluggishness of abdominal organs, which in turn impedes blood circulation, causing a feeling of despondency, confusion, headaches, constipation, chronic fatigue and neurasthenia (swaying of the body when you stand with your closed eyes).

This posture is corrective and remedial in nature for boosting physical coordination and balance as well as promotes mental poise and spiritual elevation.

This seemingly simple posture, however, makes you acutely aware of the importance of sense faculties such as sight and breath. As in this case, you will observe that as soon as you close your eyes the body will sway a little and you will need to manage your breath in a subtle way to steady it.

Method of Practice

Starting Position
1. Stand erect keeping your hands at your sides and your feet together. Check that your abdomen is held slightly inwards or in normal contour, your pelvis gently tucked in, chest lifted slightly but shoulders relaxed.
2. Gaze at any one point straight ahead, keeping your mind calm and body relaxed.

Steps
3. Fold both your hands in namaskara mudra and place them in front of your chest.
4. Keep your shoulders and elbows relaxed.
5. Close your eyes and observe your breath or fix your gaze at any one point.
6. Stay in the position for at least five minutes, taking it up to ten minutes. The aim is to hold your body motionless not allowing it to sway when your eyes are closed.

   Note: In case you find you cannot maintain balance and experience swaying of the body

   ► you can stand with your feet a little apart to gain balance;
   ► you may keep your eyes open to stare at a fixed point ahead of you, and
   ► you can place your body weight on the ball of the feet near the big toes.

Posture Release
7. Slowly open your eyes and gently lower your hands to assume the starting position.
8. Maintain your mental calm for as long as possible.

Limitations / Contraindications

1. If you are suffering from acute arthritis (lower limbs), varicose veins and hypotension you should not stand for a long time.
2. In case you have vertigo, keep your eyes open and the gaze fixed and keep your feet a little apart as there may be a chance of toppling over.

Benefits

Physical

1. It aids stance through coordination of the neuroskeletal system.
2. Physical steadiness arises through control over the voluntary muscular movements.

Therapeutic

1. It corrects postural defects.

Psychological

1. It calms your mind and relaxes the nerves.
2. Slow and rhythmic breathing in this position induces a meditative state.
3. It improves concentration, as the mind remains aware.

Muscles Involved
1. All postural muscles
2. Elbow flexors
3. Wrist extensors

Vajrasana—The Adamant Posture*

My strengthened body ensures a powerful mind.

This asana is inspired by the mythical weapon wielded by Lord Indra. It is also known to have the power of a thunderbolt, having immense force. It enables the development of bala, strength, but of a divine nature.

Symbolically, it represents firmness of spiritual prowess. Vajrasana is the posture that enhances strength, concentration, stability and virility.

It is the only posture that can be practised after a meal.

Method of Practice

Starting Position
1. Assume a kneeling position on a mat with your knees touching each other. Let your toes touch each other and the heels remain apart.

Steps
2. Lower your body and sit comfortably on the hollow formed by your toes and heels. If you are a beginner use your hands to lower yourself down. You may use a soft mat initially.
3. Hold your body erect and your head, neck and body in a natural line, the abdomen held in normal contour.
4. Place your hands upon your knees with your palms facing downwards.
5. Close your eyes and passively observe your breath or keep your gaze fixed at one point. Sit for around 5 to 10 minutes.

Posture Release

6. Slowly open your eyes and gently assume the starting position, unwind your legs and gently stretch your legs forward as in a sitting position.

Limitations / Contraindications

1. Acute arthritis.
2. Very high or low blood pressure.
3. When you are feeling low or depressed this posture helps if you keep your eyes open and the awareness directed at keeping your body still.

Benefits

Physical

1. There is a correction of the posture as the spine is automatically held erect.
2. It stretches the thighs, calves, ankles and hips.
3. It stretches the spine.

Therapeutic

1. It offers uniform postural fixity and corrects postural defects.
2. It improves blood circulation to the abdominal region thus helping improve digestion.
3. It is beneficial if you suffer from sciatica or severe lower back problems or constipation or stomach disorder or digestive problems or acidity.

4. Flexibility of the lower limbs develops.
5. The generative organs are toned along with toning of the muscles of the hips, thighs and calves.
6. It provides relief from urinary problems.

Psychological
1. This posture calms the mind and relaxes the nerves.
2. Slow and rhythmic breathing in this position can induce a meditative state.
3. Awareness of thoughts and mindfulness increases as you learn to be in the present.

Muscles Involved
1. Ankle plantar flexors
2. Ankle dorsi, knee, hip and shoulder joint flexors

Vrshasana—The Bull Posture*

My senses run amok; skilfully I bring them within my control.

Though the name sounds inappropriate for a meditative posture, it represents controlled and regulated virility and the management and mastery over your ever-fluctuating thoughts.

The formation of the posture by placing your legs in a certain way protects and strengthens your groin and excretory muscles.

Method of Practice

Starting Position
1. Sit erect on a mat with your feet outstretched.

Steps
2. Bend your right leg inwards at the knee and place the foot very close to your left hip, toes pointing outwards.
3. Take your left leg, bending it inwards at your knee, cross it over your right knee and place the foot near the outside of your right hip. Check to see that the knees are aligned on top of the other as far as possible.

4. Clasp the fingers of your hands or one hand on the other and place them on your upper knee. Keep your body erect and shoulders relaxed.
5. Close your eyes and watch your breath.
6. You can repeat by reversing the position of the legs.

Posture Release
7. Unclasp your fingers and release your legs to return to the starting position.

Limitations / Contraindications
1. Acute arthritis.
2. Very high or low blood pressure. When you are feeling low or depressed this posture helps if your eyes are kept open and the awareness is directed at keeping your body still.

Benefits

Physical
1. It stretches your thighs, calves, ankles and hips.
2. It stretches your spine.

Therapeutic
1. It improves your digestion.
2. It maintains uprightness of your spine during meditation.

Psychological
1. It calms your mind.
2. It builds awareness of the body and mind.

Muscles Involved
1. Thigh abductors

Virasana—The Heroic Posture*

> *I become strong and strengthen my resolve.*

Though this posture is called the Heroic Posture, it is similar to Vajrasana both in the context of name and effect. It strengthens resolve and brings about steadfastness. This pose is taken by Lord Hanuman, the valiant devotee of Lord Rama when seated at the feet of his lord and whose valour and equipoise were an extraordinary combination.

Method of Practice

Starting Position
1. Assume a kneeling position on a mat with your knees and feet touching each other.

Steps
2. Sit in Vajrasana.
3. Bend your right knee and place your foot closely next to your left knee, checking that your toes are in line with the left knee. Balance the hip and upper body as you are now sitting on one foot.
4. Place the left hand on your left knee and the right hand on your right knee.
5. Keep your head straight.
6. Close your eyes and watch your breath.
7. You can change the leg positions to the opposite.

Posture Release
8. Slowly bring both your legs to the kneeling position.

9. Sit on one side and straighten the legs one at a time or both together.
10. Or, relax the legs in a way comfortable for you.

Limitations / Contraindications
1. Severe arthritis and/or stiffness of the lower limbs.
2. Acute knee pain.

Benefits
Physical
1. It stretches your hips, thighs, knees, ankles and feet.

Therapeutic
1. It improves circulation and relieves tired legs. It strengthens the foot arches and relieves pain from flat feet.

Psychological
1. It creates a sense of well-being, emotional stability and improves confidence.

Muscles Involved
1. Flexors and extensors of the vertebral column
2. Knee flexors and extensors

Yoni Mudra—The Womb Posture*

The eternal sounds of the universe resonate within my entire being.

The word 'yoni' means womb. In yoga and Indian philosophical thought, the yoni is symbolically the divine womb (Brahmayoni) or the cosmic golden womb (Hiranyagarbha) from which the entire cosmic universe has emerged.

Yoni Mudra enables sense withdrawal. The senses which are normally directed towards the world are directed inwards to experience the universe within.

It is an imitation of a tortoise who withdraws all its limbs inside its shell the moment it experiences external stimulation. Yoni Mudra provides the best psycho-physical method for inducing and developing neutrality under undesirable surroundings.

Method of Practice

Starting Position
1. Sit in Sukhasana.

Steps
2. Place your thumbs on the tragus (the tiny flap at the entry of ear canal on the anterior side). Gently press inwards closing your ear canal.
3. Place your index fingers lightly on your closed lashes.
4. Now put your middle fingers lightly on the outside of your nostrils, the ring fingers above your upper lip and little fingers below your lower lip/chin.
5. Ensure that your elbows are parallel to the ground.
6. Concentrate on your breath or listen to the sounds within your body while in this mudra.
7. Stay in this mudra for at least 5 to 10 minutes.

Note: In case your hands get weary when staying for a longer duration you may, if need be, lower your elbows keeping the hands and fingers in their respective positions.

Limitations / Contraindications
1.   Psychiatric disorders

Benefits
It is a psycho-physical technique that helps your mind to withdraw its senses from being outwards and reduces the unnecessary chattering of your mind to provide that pause needed for a change of perception.

Antaranga Trataka—Internal Object Awareness*

Gathering the wayward forces within;
I develop absolute concentration.

Antaranga Trataka is a meditative technique where the aim is to focus all your attention on an internal space. It helps to begin the process of dharana leading to dhyana.

Method of Practice

Starting Position
1.   Choose a dark room (which is not pitch-dark but not too brightly lit).
2.   Sit erect but comfortably in any meditative posture or on a straight-backed chair.

Steps
3.   Close your eyes. Let your awareness go to the area within your body you wish to focus on like the place between the centre of your eyebrows, heart region or any other place.
4.   Maintain your focus and awareness at that chosen place for as long as you comfortably can. It can be from 2 to 10 minutes.

Posture Release
5.   When you wish to release the concentration, cup or palm your eyes and slowly open them.

Limitations / Contraindications
None.

Benefits
This technique helps in improving your concentration and developing quietude.

HANSAJI J. YOGENDRA'S SAHAJ BHAVASANAS

Over years of teaching yoga to people of different age groups, body types, with varying ailments and temperaments, Hansaji J. Yogendra developed several practices, which are based in the yoga tradition, yet modified to suit the beginner as well as the advanced seeker.

Her practices are called Sahaj Bhavasanas. The term 'sahaj' means simplicity, spontaneity and ease. These asanas create awareness of the body, the breath and keeps the mind attentive. Their practice results in a leaner and stronger body, builds immunity against several infectious ailments and keeps it fit and youthful.

Some of them function as warm-up stretches, popularly known as Laghu Vyayama (light exercises) or Sukshma Vyayama (subtle exercises), which are imperative to any asana session. However, the main difference between the two compared to Sahaj Bhavasana is several of the latter incorporate breathing rhythms, slow and graceful movements, attitudes and attentiveness, as they are not mere exercises.

The term 'Bhavasana' epitomizes all the four bhavas. Dharma bhava is represented in the universality of practice with hardly a few limitations, jnana bhava is evident in its potential of creating immense self-awareness of body, breath and mind. Vairagya bhava is established through its versatility and finally, aishvarya bhava becomes manifest in the emergent strong mind–body complex.

On practice of these postures, you will realize that though they seem simple they have remarkable and manifold effects. They leave you energized and the muscles of your entire body are fully stretched.

Another unique feature is the inclusion of variations to several postures that can be done standing, sitting or even lying down for their benefits to be gained. Thus even the ill, handicapped or people who lead a sedentary lifestyle can experience wellness and health.

With postural awareness, breath-management and mindfulness to be instilled during practice, in the following few pages unfold these practices leading towards a path of wellness and self-discovery!

The Commencement

1. Some of these postures (1, 2 and 3) are to be practised before any asana session. They help initiate the flow of blood and energy through the body, loosen the taut muscles and are like a warm up to further intense asana practice. They provide a gentle but deep internal awakening of the sleeping musculature into action.
2. Breathing rhythms have been incorporated into the practices, which aid in energy flow to each cell.
3. Practise these postures slowly and with full awareness.
4. Though these postures are said to be done standing, most of them can be done sitting as well. The practices that can be done both sitting and standing are marked as 'SnS'. However, it must be understood that sitting is on a straight-backed chair without arms.
5. Most of these practices have no limitations for people with

reasonably good health. Even those who have certain problems can practise them as many can be done sitting and lying down. Most of them can be practised by people who have hypertension, cardiac, diabetes, orthopaedic and respiratory problems. Even the aged who cannot move about much can practise several of these variations.

The only exception would be post-surgery or specific contraindications by a physician.

6. Several postures are intended for those who wish to intensify their practice and experience something different.

The Sahaj Bhavasanas are classified under the seven following headings.

The first three sections can also be used as warm-up practices.

1. Sahaj Kantha Bhavasanas (SKB): Postures for head and neck (SnS)—eleven variations
2. Sahaj Bajubandha Bhavasanas (SBB): Postures for shoulders, arms, hands and fingers (SnS)—twelve variations
3. Sahaj Kati Madhya Bhavasanas (SKMB): Postures for torso, hips, toes, feet and knees—(SnS) and lying down:
   a. Torso flows—three variations
   b. The hips, toes, feet and knees variations for standing, sitting and lying down
4. Sahaj Adhara Bhavasanas (SAB): Wall/window support movements for:
   a. Arms, shoulders and back
   b. Shoulders
   c. Waist
   d. Hips, thighs and legs—three variations
5. Baithak Sahaj Bhavasanas (BSB): Sitting postures:
   a. Sitting on the ground—six variations
6. Baithak Chalana Sahaj Bhavasanas (BCSB): Hip walking, sitting on the ground, three variations
7. Shayan Sahaj Bhavasanas (ShSB): Lying down for the arms, shoulders, torso/waist, hips and legs

a. Simple lying down—three variations
b. Torso curves—five variations
c. Lying on the stomach—three variations

Sahaj Kantha Bhavasanas (SKB): Postures for Head and Neck (SnS)

All these practices are excellent if you are working on computers for long or have a desk job.

They can be done sitting at the desk itself, but it is always better to stand if you can.

These form the first in the three series of warm-up practices for everyone before commencing an asana session.

Starting position for all variations:

1. Standing: Stand with your feet slightly apart or at a one-foot distance.
2. Sitting: Sit erect on a straight-backed chair without arms. In case you do not have a straight-backed chair without arms, sit firmly on the edge of the chair taking care you do not topple over.

Hold your head straight and hands at your sides or on the thighs.

Remember to keep your abdomen tucked in (not constricted) and shoulders squared so that an erect posture is maintained.

Variation 1

1. As you inhale, gently allow your head to drop towards your right shoulder without lifting your shoulder.
2. Exhaling, bring it back to the centre. Drop it to the left shoulder in the same way and return to the centre.

Variation 2

1. While inhaling, tilt your head backwards as far as you can without moving your shoulders or the body and gaze upwards and backwards at the ceiling.

2. While exhaling, bring your head down towards your throat, tucking your chin in to the throat cavity.
3. Inhaling, return to the centre.

Variation 3

1. Inhaling, turn your head to look far right and behind. Exhaling, return to the centre.
2. Repeat on the other side.

Variation 4

All the following steps are done in one gentle continuous motion.

1. Inhaling, drop your head to the right, taking it back rotating your head from right to left to reach your left shoulder side and as you exhale, your head returns up straight. Please note that there is no forward bending of your head. Repeat starting from the opposite side. This is a clockwise and anti-clockwise rotation of the head.

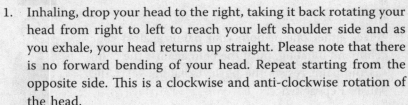

Variation 5

1. Clasp your hands, placing them behind your head and elbows in the front.
2. Inhaling, push your head back against your palms as the palms try to push the head ahead.
3. Hold for five seconds and relax the pressure. Repeat twice.

Variation 6

1. Place your palm at your right temple and inhaling, push your head into the palm, the palm resisting this push. Exhaling, relax the push.
2. Repeat on the opposite side.
3. Repeat on both sides.

Variation 7

1. Place your palms against your forehead and inhaling, push your head into the palms as the palms push it back. Exhaling, relax the push. Repeat twice.

Variation 8

1. Place either one or both your palms against your chin and inhaling, push the chin against the palm as the palm resists the push. Exhaling, relax the push. Repeat twice.

Variation 9

1. Place your chin in the palms and inhaling, push the chin into the palms as the palms resist the push and press upwards. Exhaling, relax the push. Repeat twice.

Variation 10

This variation is done standing.

1. Stand with your hands clasped close behind on your hip.
2. Square your shoulders and push your hands and shoulders down.
3. Inhaling, look up till your chin is stretched and pointing up at the ceiling.

4. While exhaling, bring your head straight and relax your shoulders. Repeat twice.

Variation 11

1. While standing or sitting point and push your chin out as you inhale.
2. Exhaling, relax your chin. Repeat twice.

Sahaj Bajubandha Bhavasanas (SBB): Postures for Shoulders, Arms, Hands and Fingers (SnS)

All these practices are excellent if you are working on computers for long or have a desk job. These are also part of the warm-up practices.

Variation 1

This posture is best done standing. In case you are sitting, spread your knees so that there is place to stretch your hands downwards.

1. Clasp your hands loosely clasped in the front.
2. As you inhale, push your clasped hands down as far as you can stretch them without bending forward. Keep your shoulders fixed, tucking your elbows into your waist. Stay there for 5 seconds.
3. Exhaling, relax your hands. Repeat twice.

Variation 2

1. Place your fingertips of both your hands in front of the chest.
2. As you inhale, try to press against your fingertips against each other forcefully. Hold for 5 seconds.
3. Exhaling, relax the pressure. Repeat twice.

Variation 3

Phase I

1. Keeping your hands close at the sides, while inhaling, lift your shoulders as high up as you can towards your ears.
2. Exhaling, relax your shoulders.
3. Repeat this motion twice.

Phase II

1. Place your hands on your hips and keep your head and body erect.
2. Inhaling, take both your shoulders back keeping your body still.
3. Exhaling, relax your shoulders. Repeat twice.

Phase III

1. You can perform these exercises with hands at the sides or placed on your hips.
2. Perform as a single shoulder rotation. Inhaling, as you lift and take one shoulder backwards and exhaling, as you bring it back to normal.
3. Repeat with the other shoulder.

Phase IV

Practise the same with both shoulders following the same breathing rhythm.

Phase V

Practise shoulder rotations taking the rotation from back, down and then upwards while inhaling and as you exhale bring the shoulders down.

Note: You can perform this shoulder rotation with each shoulder separately too.

Variation 4

1. Clasp your hands at the back at the normal hip level.
2. As you inhale, lift your clasped hands as high as you can from behind, keeping your shoulders down, as much as you can.
3. Simultaneously, lift your chin and head to look at the ceiling.
4. Exhaling, relax. Repeat twice.

Variation 5

1. Place your fingers on your shoulders with your elbows meeting in the front.
2. As you inhale, begin a movement of raising your elbows in the front, separating and rising up, going backwards and down, coming to the front in the starting position.
3. Now begin the opposite movement from Step 1 while inhaling, separate your elbows and begin moving them downwards, backwards and up; exhaling, return to the starting position.

Variation 6

1. With your hands at the sides, begin lifting your right hand up from the front as you inhale, taking it up and bending it at the elbow to go over, behind the left shoulder.
2. Simultaneously, the left hand from below goes backwards to clasp the right hand. Remain in

the position for five seconds before releasing the grasp.

3. Repeat with the opposite hands.

Note: You can also practise this posture seated on a chair.

Variation 7

1. Take both your hands behind from below and try to form a Namaskara Mudra at the back.
2. Stay in the position for five seconds.

Variation 8

Phase I

1. Press your palms in Namaskara Mudra a little away from your chest.
2. Inhaling, exert pressure and exhaling, release the pressure. Keep your shoulders relaxed during this practice.

Phase II

1. Same as Phase I.
2. Press your palms together, keep your abdomen tucked in and inhaling, raise your pressed palms together above your head.
3. Exhaling, return to the starting position. Relax the pressure and bring your hands down.

Phase III

1. Continue from Phase II, Step 2. Exhale and relax your shoulders and hands while your hands are still above your head.
2. Inhaling, press your palms and bend your elbows backwards till the fingers point down behind the head.

3. Exhaling, release the pressure, take your hands up, the palms still in Namaskara Mudra and bring them to the starting position (Step 1 of Phase I).

Phase IV
1. Start in the same position as Step 1, Phase I.
2. Pressing your palms, keep your body motionless and move your hands to the right.
3. Return to the centre.
4. Repeat on the left side.

Variation 9

1. Stand with your feet a little apart and your hands raised straight in the front at shoulder level, palms together.
2. Try to join your forearms and in this position bend your elbows to raise the palms, fingers pointing at the ceiling.
3. Straighten your hands. Repeat this movement for three to four times.

Variation 10

Phase I
1. While inhaling, entwine your fingers at the chest and stretch out your hands.
2. While exhaling, relax the stretch.

Phase II
1. While inhaling, stretch your hand and entwined fingers as you point your palm outwards.
2. Exhaling, relax the stretch.

Phase III

1. Repeat Phase I and Phase II while you take your hands up above your head.

Phase IV

1. Repeat Phase I and Phase II while you take both your hands to the right and then to the left.

Phase V

1. Keep your hands outstretched at the shoulder level with your right palm facing out and up.
2. While inhaling, with the left hand fingers push the right hand fingers behind as much as you comfortably can.
3. Exhaling, relax. Repeat with the opposite hand.

Variation 11

Phase I

1. Stretch both your hands to the shoulder level with your palms facing down and fingers as wide apart as possible.
2. While inhaling, take your hands to the respective sides and as far back without tilting your body backwards.
3. Exhaling, return to the front.

Variation 12

1. Stretch your hands out at the shoulder level and gently clench your fists.
2. Keeping the hands straight, perform wrist rotation both clockwise and anti-clockwise. Repeat twice.

Sahaj Kati Madhya Bhavasanas (SKMB): Postures for the Torso, Hips, Toes, Feet and Knees (SnS) and Lying Down

Torso flows: Variations for the torso include:

Variation 1

SnS

This variation can be done both standing and sitting. In this practice, the back is stretched and the abdomen is held in.

If you are practising this variation sitting, it is best done sitting on the ground with legs spread apart.

In case you wish to practise sitting on a chair, firmly sit on the edge of a straight-backed chair, preferably wooden (plastic is too lightweight and prone to toppling) without upholstery. A dining chair without armrests is ideal. Keep your knees a little apart, abdomen tucked in. Place your heels flat on the floor if you are a beginner. You can try to raise your heels with toes on the floor.

1. Sit on a chair with your hips firmly fixed, but at the edge.
2. Clasp your hands above your head, holding the head with your forearms. Keep your legs a foot apart and feet parallel to each other.
3. Inhale and tuck in your abdomen and as you exhale, in one continuous flowing movement bend down to the right from the waist to the centre, to the left and up to the centre
4. Repeat such clockwise and anti-clockwise movements twice. Check that during the entire torso flow, your head and hands move together.

Variation 2

1. Sit on a chair with your hips firmly fixed but at the edge.
2. Inhaling, raise both your arms above your head and as you exhale, bring them down in a smooth sweep to touch your toes. In case you cannot touch your toes, go as far down as you can without toppling over.
3. Keep your left hand fixed on your opposite foot, inhale and as you exhale contract your abdomen, twist your torso to the right and simultaneously take your right hand up to a point towards the ceiling as you look up at your raised hand.

Variation 3

Phase I

1. Stand with your legs two and half feet distance apart.
2. Place your palms on your hips as shown.
3. Tighten the hip muscles, inhaling bend backwards gently.
4. Exhaling, return to the upright position.

Note: Do not practise this variation if you have hypertension, cardiac ailments and vertigo.

Hips and legs: Variations for the hips and legs generally include squats, leg lifts and lunges as they are good for the hips and legs, especially the thighs. However, in this section new practices are described, which are very effective.

Variation 1

1. Stand with your legs a little apart, hands at the sides, elbows bent a little or placed on the waist.
2. Take your right leg back as though you are ready to sprint or run. The left leg will be bent. The body also will be in a slight angle. Refer to the picture.
3. In this posture, the leg in the front which is stationary will be exercised, thus with the body weight on the left leg, bring the right leg forwards and upwards with the knee bent and stretch it out in the front. In case you cannot balance, spread your hands out.
4. Hold this position with the weight on the left leg for a count of ten.

5. Extend your right leg and hold till a count of ten.
6. Bring your right foot down to the starting position.
7. Repeat with the other leg.

Note: In this posture, the emphasis is on the slightly bent leg with a foot on the floor, which takes on the entire body weight.

Variation 2

1. Stand with your feet slightly apart and hand on the hips and throughout this practice keep your knees slightly bent.
2. Keeping the knees slightly bent, thrust your right leg forward and up with your toes pointed. Hold the position for a count of ten.
3. Bring your leg down and take it straight up to the right, keeping your toes pointed. Hold for a count of ten.

4. Bring the leg back to the centre.
5. Repeat all steps on the opposite side.
6. You can practise both the forward and sidewards thrust of the leg in one continuous movement, once you can manage stability on one leg.

Other variations for exercising the hips and thighs have been given as Hansaji's variations to Hastapadangushthasana.

Toes, feet and knees: The toes and feet are rarely given much importance in any scheme of exercise. However, the toes and feet enable support of the body, are the aids in balanced walking, they hold a number of nerve endings and all the organs of the body are represented in the soles of the feet. Proper care and exercise of the toes and feet is imperative.

For toes and feet in the standing position: Following are the variations.

Variation 1

1. Take both your hands up above your head, as you inhale, raise the hands to the ceiling (you can keep your fists clenched or leave your palms open), and simultaneously raise the heels to stand on your toes.
2. Breathing normally, walk on your toes as if in a approximately 200-square-foot room once or twice.
3. Relax. Do not overdo this practice.

For toes and feet while sitting (some of these can be done lying down if one is unable to sit and practise for any reasons): Following are the variations.

Variation 1

Keep your legs straight and simultaneously point your toes of one foot and flex the other set of toes. Keep up this alternate movement for around ten times.

Variation 2

Keeping both your legs and feet together and knees straight, rotate feet clockwise and anti-clockwise of both the legs together. Make sure you make complete movements of pointing and flexing the toes.

Variation 3

1. Hold your toes of one leg with all your fingers as shown.
2. Push your toes down with all your strength and at the same time let your fingers resist that push.

   Note: You can practise with one foot at a time or both together.

Variation 4

1. Keep your legs together with your feet resting down.
2. Lift your heels off the floor. Remain in the position for ten seconds.

Variation 5

1. Spread your knees and feet apart, lift the heels up.
2. Inhaling, raise both your hands and join the palms above your head.

For the toes and feet while lying down: The following practices are excellent if due to some reason you cannot stand or sit and yet wish to maintain blood flow and flexibility to the lower extremities of your body.

Variation 1

1. Lie on the floor with your feet together and your hands partially tucked under your hips, palms facing down.
2. Tighten your abdomen while pointing the toes, slowly lift both your legs off the floor as high up as you can, or till they are at a right angle to the body.
3. Hold for ten seconds.
4. Pointing your toes again towards the ceiling slowly lower the legs down taking care that your lower back is well supported by your hands.

Note: In case you cannot practise with both your legs together you can alternate the legs taking them up one at a time.

Variation 2

Follow the same steps as Variation 1 except instead of raising your legs high, the legs are raised just about three inches off the floor.

For the knees: Following is the variation.

Variation 1

1. Lie on a mat with both your legs together and hands at the shoulder level.
2. Bend both your knees and twist your lower body so that your left knee touches the floor on the right side.

   Note: You can also make movements of the knee by pressing your knee down, relaxing it and then again pressing it down.

Sahaj Adhara Bhavasanas (SAB) (Wall/Window Support Movements)

All the following Sahaj Bhavasanas correct faulty posture, strengthen the arms, shoulders and help in toning the hips and thighs. It is best to choose a wall rather than a window unless specified. Avoid using a chair as a support.

For the arms, shoulders and back: Following are the variations.

Variation 1

1. Stand erect against a wall, feet together, head, shoulders, upper back, hips, legs and heels touching the wall.
2. Raise your arm up above your head while inhaling, palms facing towards the wall and touch them flat on the wall.
3. Remain in the position breathing normally for ten seconds.
4. Return to starting position as you exhale.
   For the shoulders: Following is the variation.

Variation 2

1. Stand against the wall as above. Keep your abdomen tucked in.
2. As you inhale deeply, raise your arms from the sides till your shoulder level.
3. Turn your palms to face the wall and press them flat on it.
4. Exhaling, bring your hands down.
5. Continue this movement continuously for five rounds.

For the waist: Following is the variation.
1. Stand in the same way as above.
2. Raise your arms to shoulder level and tuck your abdomen in.
3. Keeping the arms unmoving, bend on the right as far down as you can, checking that your body is touching the wall during the entire movement.

For the hips, thighs and legs: Following is the variation.

Variation 1

1. Stand erect, put your feet a foot apart and parallel to each other, facing a wall arm distance away.

2. Place both your palms flat on the wall.
3. Inhaling, lift your right leg from behind.
4. Bend your leg at the knee and bring your heel close to your hips, squeezing the hamstring muscles.
5. Exhaling, straighten your knee and bring the leg down.
6. Repeat with the other leg. Repeat ten times with each leg.

Variation 2

1. Stand about three feet away from the wall or windowsill with your feet a little apart.
2. Bend from your hips to touch the wall ahead, the upper body horizontal and parallel to the ground. Keep your back and legs straight.
3. Inhaling, raise one leg straight up from behind.
4. Exhaling, bring your leg down.
5. Repeat with the opposite leg.

Variation 3

1. Stand erect against a wall with your feet together and your head, shoulders, upper back, hips, legs and heels touching the wall. Keep your abdomen tucked in.
2. Rise up on your toes as you inhale and as you exhale glide down against the wall to come to a full squatting position. (You may outstretch your hands as shown in the picture.)
3. Stay in the position for ten seconds, breathing normally.
4. While inhaling, rise on your toes and exhaling bring your heels down.

For the hips, thighs and legs lying down: Following is the variation.

Variation 4

1. Place the mat such that the length is at 90 degrees to a wall.
2. Lie down on the mat with your knees bent and feet close to the wall. Keep your hands at the sides. Refer to the picture.
3. Take your feet and place them against the wall so that the lower legs are parallel to the ground.
4. Inhaling, contract your hip muscles and lift the hips off the floor as high up as you can, moving the feet up the wall, one at a time, as high up as you can go. You can use the hands to support the hips.
5. Exhaling, relax the contraction and lower the hips to the starting position.

Baithak Sahaj Bhavasanas (Sitting Postures)

These two sections of sitting (and lying down if unable to practise sitting) postures are extremely effective. Anybody can practise them unless they are out of surgery, there is an injury or any similar complications.

These postures can be practised by everyone who can sit and move their limbs. They are powerful though done sitting. Choose a straight-backed chair without arms.

They can also be practised by an advanced practitioner being very aware of every muscle being moved and stretched.

For a hip stretch when sitting on the ground: Following is the variation.

Variation 1

1. Sit on the floor with both your legs outstretched and together.
2. Bend your right knee to touch the foot to the inner left thigh.
3. While exhaling, contract your abdomen and lift the bent right leg off the floor as high up as you can using your hands. Hold the position for six seconds suspending the breath. In case you cannot suspend the breath, breathe normally and hold the position for six seconds.
4. While inhaling, bring your leg down.
5. Repeat with the other leg.

For the hips, abdomen and upper thigh: Following is the variation.

Variation 2

Phase I

1. Sit on the floor with both your legs outstretched and together.
2. Place your palms flat on the ground near your hips for support.
3. Contract your abdomen (try not to lean backwards) as you exhale, pointing your right toe, lift the right leg straight up as high as you can.
4. Inhaling, bring the leg down.
5. Repeat with the opposite leg.

Phase II

1. Repeat steps as in previous variations from 1 to 3.
2. With your leg held up, swing it to the right and bring it back to centre in one motion.
3. Inhaling, bring your leg down.
4. Repeat with the opposite leg.

Phase III

1. Sit in the same way as above.
2. Contract your abdomen, tighten the hips and as you exhale, lift both your legs off the floor together and swing them apart in one motion, bring them back to the centre.
3. Inhaling, put your legs down.

Phase IV

1. Sit on the floor with both your legs as wide apart as you can.
2. Place your palms on the floor next to your hips, leaning backwards.
3. Contract your abdomen, tighten your hips and as you exhale, lift both your legs straight off the floor. Stay in the position for six seconds suspending your breath.
4. Inhaling, bring your legs down.

Note: Phase III of this practice is contraindicated for those with any back problems, weak abdomen, hernia and those who have had surgery.

For a groin stretch: Following is the variation.

Variation 3

1. Sit on the floor with both your legs as far apart as you can.
2. Inhaling, raise your hands from the front till shoulder level.
3. Exhaling, contract your abdomen and bend forward so that your hand touches the floor in front, keeping your head locked in-between the arms.
4. Continue to stretch your hand further and try to touch your forehead or chin down on the floor.
5. Inhaling, raise the head off the floor, keep your head locked in between the arms till your hands are at shoulder level.
6. Exhaling, bring your hands to the sides and lift your head up.

Variation 4

1. Sit in the same way as in Variation 3.
2. Interlace your fingers behind your head.
3. Tuck your abdomen in and bend laterally to the right. It is not important to touch the floor with your elbow but to check that you do not tilt forwards or backwards.
4. Repeat on the other side.
5. Repeat continuously for ten repetitions.

Note: This is excellent for all the abdominal muscles.

Variation 5

1. Sit with both your legs outstretched and together.
2. Raise both your hands to shoulder level.
3. Adjusting your weight by leaning a little backwards, bend your right knee to tuck it under the right hip. In case you cannot do this without support, use your hands to help tuck the right knee under the right hip.
4. Remain in the position for ten seconds.
5. Release your leg and repeat with the other leg.

Note: Do not practise this if you have severe or moderate arthritis.

Variation 6

1. Sit in Vajrasana.
2. Bend a little forward and place both your palms on the floor near your knees.
3. Take your right leg from under the hip straight at the back, keeping it steady.
4. Your back will be slightly arched. Keep your head straight.
5. Release your leg to return to the starting position.
6. Repeat with the other leg.

Note: Do not practise this if you have severe or moderate arthritis.

Baithak Chalana Sahaj Bhavasana (Hip Walking)

In order to practise hip walking, choose wooden or tile flooring. It cannot be done on carpeted flooring.

> Note: In this practice, you will be using the strength of your abdomen and lower back.

> Caution: Avoid this practice if you have a weak back or any problems with the abdominal area.

Variation 1

Hip Walking in One Place
1. Sit on the floor with both your legs together and outstretched. Keep your hands in a walking stance. Keep your abdomen tucked in.
2. Lift your right hip as though you are going to move with it.
3. Keep the hip down and lift the left hip up and put it down.
4. Continue this alternate movement of the hips.

Variation 2

Hip Walking—Moving Forward

1. Sit on the floor with both your legs together and outstretched. Keep your hands in a walking stance. Keep your abdomen tucked in.
2. Begin moving using your hips as though you are walking with your hips.

Variation 3

Hip Walking Going Behind

1. Sit in the same way as in Variation 2.
2. Keeping your abdomen tucked in, move your hips back and forth in a way that you are moving backwards.

Shayan Sahaj Bhavasanas (ShSB): Postures for Arms, Shoulders, Hips and Legs while Lying Down

Simple lying down postures: These practices have been specially modified for those who cannot stand or sit for any reason.

Variation 1

1. Lie down on the floor and turn over on your right, making a pillow of your right hand and resting your head on it. Try and keep your body straight and abdomen tucked in. The left hand should rest on the left thigh.
2. Inhaling, raise your left hand up straight towards the ceiling and close to your head. Make a wide rotation of your hand and while exhaling, return to the starting position. Repeat twice with each hand on both sides.

Variation 2

1. In the same starting position as above, inhaling, raise your left hand straight towards the ceiling and swing it backwards to touch it on the floor behind.
2. As you exhale, swinging it in an arc, bring it to touch the floor in the front, keeping your hand straight. You can also take the top leg behind as shown in the picture.
3. Inhaling, take the hand up and exhaling bring it to rest on your thigh. Repeat on the opposite side.

Variation 3

This variation involves a series of practices.

1. Lie straight on your back with hands flat on the ground at shoulder level and elbows bent to point up. Refer to the picture shown.
2. While exhaling, bend your elbow to bring your hands down and as you inhale take the hands up. Repeat twice.
3. Now placing your body weight on your forearms and elbow, hips and legs fixed to the ground, as you inhale lift your upper body, chest, neck off the floor. Your head should be touching the floor with your chin pointing upwards.
4. While exhaling, lower your body down.
5. Finish off this series by relaxing your hands. Keep your legs

slightly apart. Inhaling, turn your feet outwards and exhaling, point your feet inwards. Repeat twice.

The torso curves: You just have to try these out to experience how effective they are.

Variation 1

1. Lie on your back with your legs and feet together and hands at the side.
2. Raise both your hands and take them above your head to rest straight and flat on the floor, arms close to the ears.
3. Curve your upper body from the waist to the right as much as you can.
4. Now curve your lower body, from the waist down, one leg at a time, beginning with moving the right leg and bringing the left leg closer to it. The body will make a 'C' formation.
5. Stay in this position for 10 to 30 seconds and try to intensify the curve, taking care that the body or hips are not lifted.
6. Return slowly to the centre and repeat on the opposite side.

Variation 2

1. Lie on your right side, resting your head on the pillow formed by the right arm. Keep your legs straight with your left leg resting on the right leg.
2. Gradually begin taking both the legs in the same position backwards. The body will form a 'C' shape. Remain in this position for 10 to 30 seconds.
3. Return to the centre, turn to lie on your left side and repeat the practice.

Variation 3

1. Lie on your right side resting your head on the pillow formed by your right hand. Your left leg should rest on your right.
2. Keeping the right leg unmoving take your left leg as far back as you can and remain in the position for ten seconds.
3. Bend your left leg at the knee towards the hips and squeeze the hamstring muscles, staying there for ten seconds.
4. Straighten the leg and return to the centre.
5. Repeat on the opposite side.

Variation 4

1. Lie on your back with your legs spread about two feet distance apart and hands at the sides.

2. Exhaling, contract your abdomen and hips and lift both your legs off the floor.
3. Remain in the position for 10 to 30 seconds, breathing normally.
4. Inhaling, relax by taking your legs down.

Variation 5

1. Lie flat on your back.
2. Bring the soles of both your feet together as close to the groin as possible. Use your hands to bring your feet close to the groin if necessary.
3. Inhaling, raise both your hands above your head, stretched and flat on the ground.
4. Remain in this position practising abdominal breathing for 20 to 30 seconds.
5. Exhaling, bring your hands to the sides and release your legs.

Lying on the stomach: This posture includes three variations.

Variation 1

1. Lie on your stomach, chin resting on the back of your palms which are placed together and elbows down towards the chest. Refer to the picture. Keep your legs and feet together, toes pointed.
2. Putting weight on your palms while inhaling, lift the entire

abdomen off the floor, straightening the arms and looking up towards the ceiling.

3. While exhaling, bring your torso down.

Variation 2

1. Lying on your stomach with your legs and feet together, rest your chin in your palms.
2. Inhaling, raise your right foot straight up and bend at the knee towards the hips.
3. Exhaling, straighten your leg and bring it down.
4. Repeat with the other leg.

Variation 3

1. Lying on your stomach with your hands outstretched on the floor above your head, keep your legs about a foot distance apart.
2. Without lifting your hands, roll your body as much as possible to the right and then to the left. Use the strength of your core (abdomen) to help you roll.

Note: The rolling will be very little as your hands remain in place.

THE CULTURAL ASANAS

The form of the body moves in unison with the breath,
the mind so follows.
The body–breath–mind are in perfect harmony

Cultural asanas can be practised in two ways, as dynamic and static. The dynamic mode leads to a harmony between the body, breath and mind and have to be repeated for a certain number of rounds following a specific breathing rhythm and maintain a certain number of counts. When these postures are held in the final pose for a duration of not more than two minutes, keeping the breathing normal, it is the static mode. Yogic asanas provide benefits at multiple levels, thereby enriching the physical, emotional, intellectual, spiritual and ethical dimensions of human development.

The physical body when attuned with specific breathing rhythms creates a certain mental equilibrium which in turn leads to overall health and freedom from ailments. However, the Hatha Yoga texts very clearly reveal that these physical practices must lead to spiritual growth and are not merely for physical benefit alone.

The body is constantly in motion. Each moment of our waking state is characterized by motion. Even in sleep we are moving, though unaware. The asanas are designed in a way to put the body through new formations for a small duration of time to enhance its health, capacities, energy and mental equipoise. On a more subtle level, these body formations which we call asanas create an impact on the way we think and behave.

At the physiological level, these cultural or dynamic asanas primarily help in maintaining the optimum health of the internal organs. Simultaneously, they exercise the joints and major muscle groups. They improve blood circulation, coordination of the neuromuscular system and maintain steadiness of the body. They contribute to the overall well-being.

Asanas are like daily prayer. They enrich the personality and create positive experiences.

Dynamic asanas are designed in relation to the primary structure of the body: the spine. The dynamic postures are categorized by the six spinal movements they provide.

These asanas are predominantly for

1. upward stretch of the spine;
2. sideward bending of the spine;
3. forward bending of the spine;
4. backward bending of the spine;
5. twisting of the spine and
6. inverted position of the spine.

An index of all practices has been included at the end of the book.

Choosing a series of asanas suitable to you is important. You can pick asanas and make your own series.

Ideally, an asana session is as follows. However, you can modify it to suit your personal requirements.

1. Conditioning practice.
2. Sahaj Bhavasanas series 1, 2 and 3 (preparatory and warm-up exercises).
3. Standing postures.
4. Sitting postures.
5. Lying down postures.
6. Relaxation postures culminating with Shavasana.
7. Pranayamas and kriyas like Jala Neti or Kapal Bhati can be

practised independently of any asana and pranayama.

8. You can choose to practise meditation at the end of an asana and a pranayama session or meditate independently.

For those practising yoga in the evening after tiring work hours, they may begin with relaxation asanas followed by the aforementioned sequence.

Note: Prior to commencing any session of dynamic asanas, practise it as suggested.

1. Refer to the symbol guide to check the level of difficulty.
2. In case of any medical problem, it is best to seek the advice of a physician and not to begin any series of asana practice on your own.
3. If you have a medical history, after clearance from your physician, please practise under the guidance of an expert yoga teacher or in consultation with one to avoid any injury or harm.

Other Guidelines

1. Keeping in mind the place you are in, adjust the temperature settings so that you can practise comfortably, irrespective of whether the asanas are meditative or dynamic. A well-ventilated room would be ideal in a tropical climate but it is best to adjust according to your country, climate and region. Yoga is not about torturing yourself but to elevate yourself at all levels—physical, mental and spiritual!
2. Wear comfortable clothes, preferably made from natural fabric.
3. Practise a few rounds of Sahaj Bhavasanas (series 1, 2 and 3) to warm up the body before commencing an asana session.
4. Whenever you begin any posture, check your stance. Be sure to keep your abdomen in, shoulders squared, back straight and body weight equal on both legs. Do not be rigid but also avoid any kind of slouching. It is not an army training but be confident and upright.

5. You can stay with one series or choose to practise different series of asanas on different days.
6. An entire session can be planned based on Sahaj Bhavasanas alone.
7. At the completion of the asana session, make sure to relax in any of the relaxation postures and end with Shavasana.

Note: Though these asanas are dynamic in nature you can choose to stay in the final position of some asanas for a maximum of two minutes.

Breathing Rhythms during an Asana Practice Session

Wherever inhaling and exhaling is mentioned, it is recommended you practise three seconds of inhalation and three seconds of exhalation. However, refer to the ratio guide in the section on pranayamas and reduce or increase it according to your capacity, nearer to your breathing capacity. Each individual practice may not mention the duration or ratio.

Retention of breath will be mentioned wherever required depending on the individual practice. Mostly, retention of breath will be for six seconds unless specified otherwise.

It is important to note that the three seconds inhalation is spread over the duration taken to reach the final position and not to inhale first and then get into position. It is same with exhalation.

Repetition of an Asana

The number of repetitions of an asana depends on a variety of factors. Thus for each asana we have avoided specifying the number of repetitions you can perform.

None of the traditional yoga texts discusses repetition of asanas. It was left to the teacher to decide. Hence, being subjective in nature, the numbers of repetitions have been avoided but a few guidelines are given.

1. It is important to perform the preparatory exercises, the Sahaj Bhavasanas series 1, 2 and 3, to relax and warm up the muscles.

Otherwise, you may suffer an injury such as a crick in the neck, a painful muscle pull on the back or damage the joints.

2. The time you have will determine the number of repetitions. In case on a particular day, you do not have the required time you can perform at least one to two rounds of the asanas you have chosen from each group. This will ensure each joint and muscle group is exercised.

3. If you are staying in a posture for a longer duration then only one or two repetitions is sufficient.

4. The number of asanas chosen by you will decide the number of repetitions. For example, if you have chosen fewer asanas the number of repetitions will be more compared to a large number of asanas.

5. The number of repetitions also depends on your age and health. A seventy-year-old may have the flexibility and stamina of a thirty-year-old and sometimes a thirty-year-old for some reasons may not be as fit. Thus every individual can decide the number of repetitions, sequence and which asanas they should practise.

6. There is a current trend of performing Surya Namaskara several times. At The Yoga Institute, we do not believe in the idea as the purpose of asanas is not merely for exercise but it should lead to a healthy body housing a peaceful and calm mind. Every position in the Surya Namaskara is infused with a mantra, a breathing rhythm, an emotion and an area of concentration. These bhavanas have to be cultivated along with the physical practice.

7. The number of repetitions you can perform depends on your fitness levels. They can range anywhere between three to five repetitions. If you are remaining static in some postures, repetitions may not be necessary.

Dynamic vs Static Postures

Please refer to Chapter 6, Dynamics of Movement, to decide whether you choose the dynamic version or maintain the posture in a static form for no more than two minutes in relation to the cultural postures.

At the beginning of every asana we have presented to you a bhava, an inspiring thought, so that inculcating the idea and reflecting on it during the practice will result in corresponding physical and emotional transformations.

Hansaji J. Yogendra's Variations

Along with the traditional asanas there are some unique variations to certain asanas as conceived by Hansaji J. Yogendra. Considering the erratic and sedentary lifestyles of people today, she designed several variations which could be adapted by people in their everyday routines. Some have been simplified and modified so that even those who are unable to stand or sit can gain the benefits through their practice while lying down. In fact, every person can gain benefits through their regular practice.

The Ultimate Thought before You Begin Practice

This book is principally on asanas and the other physiological practices, including pranayamas and kriyas. But the key idea is how these practices are done and their chief objectives.

Is the objective merely physical wellness or something more? Is it to master the numerous asanas, be proficient in every technique, to be able to stand upside down? Is it to move gracefully from one posture to another till the sweat drips or is it for therapy and alleviation of ailments?

Well, we may become experts of the physical forms, have a super body, be very fit, but can we maintain mental equipoise? Do we get disturbed by the ups and downs of life? Can we sit for a while without having disturbing thoughts or even for a few seconds without a thought at all?

Though this book teaches the various practices of yoga, it is not merely for physical fitness and therapy, though there are numerous therapeutic, physical and psychological benefits. The idea is to relish each action and experience the unity of the mind, breath and body.

The idea is not to jump from one posture to another, neither is it to practise the maximum number of techniques or to perform a hundred Surya Namaskaras. Physical yoga, by influencing the mind, brings about mindfulness, humility, peace, joy and a state of remaining unaffected by the multiplicity of life! Good health, wellness and fitness are by-products of yoga practice.

Keeping in mind these fundamental concepts let us embark on a journey towards self-discovery where each movement and moment results in wholesome experiences.

Surya Namaskar—The Sun Salutation**

> The one, brilliant magnificent Sun
> Nourisher and sustainer, source of all life
> The illuminator of all things, I offer my obeisance
> May that Divine energy, strength and wisdom be imparted
> unto me.

Surya Namaskar or Sun Salutation is a technique of vitalization via solar energy. Invocation and worship of the Sun was one of the first and most natural forms of expression of awe and gratitude. Sun worship is still practised as a daily ritual in many parts of India, as it is a powerful symbol of life energy.

Surya Namaskar is a series of twelve different physical movements. These movements consist of alternate backward and forward bending asanas, thereby flexing and stretching the spinal column and limbs to their maximum capacity. It massages, tones, stretches and stimulates all the muscles and vital organs of the body. It loosens up all the joints, massages the internal organs, activates the respiratory and circulatory system as well as helps all other systems of the body to function optimally. It harmonizes the whole body–mind complex.

Surya Namaskar consists of five essential aspects. All of them must be followed to gain the optimum results. They are as follows:

1. Asanas: There are twelve postures and the complete cycle consists of twenty-four movements, which have to be practised in a sequence, one after the other, with retention of each position for a few seconds, if possible.

2. Breathing: The complete cycle of Surya Namaskar is synchronized with breathing. Each posture is associated with either inhalation or exhalation or retention or suspension of breath.

3. Mantra: Each posture is accompanied by a specific mantra repeated either silently or loudly. These mantras add to the benefits. Before integrating these mantras, it is advisable to first perfect the postures and synchronize them with breathing.

4. Awareness: Awareness is a crucial part of this practice through which its effects are experienced at the cellular level. It increases the capacity of concentration and chanting brings about harmony at all levels.

5. Relaxation: For beginners, after completing about three rounds, relaxation is important.

Note: 1. You may chant the mantras mentally. If you are chanting aloud it will be difficult to synchronize with the breathing rhythm but it is possible with practice.

2. Once your hands touch the floor in Posture 3, till you reach Posture 10, the hands remain fixed in the same place.

Method of Practice

Posture 1: Sthita Prarthanasana—Standing Prayer Posture

1. Begin by standing erect on the front of the mat with the hands at the sides.

   ▶ Chant mantra: '*Om Mitraya Namaha*' (Salutation to the friend of All).

   ▶ Stand erect with the feet together.

   ▶ Bring palms in namaste position and place them in front of your chest.

   ▶ Relax the body, maintain normal breathing and stay for 3 seconds.

Posture 2: Hasta Uttanasana—Raised Arm Posture

   ▶ Chant mantra: '*Om Ravaye Namaha*' (Salutation to the radiant One).

- ► Inhaling, raise both your arms and bend backwards. Keep your arms close to your ears with your palms facing front.
- ► Maintain the position for 3 seconds.

Posture 3: Hasta Padasana—Hands to Legs Posture
Chant mantra: *'Om Suryaya Namaha'* (Salutation to He who initiates all activity).

- ► Exhaling, bend forward, place your palms on the floor on each side of your feet.
- ► Keeping your legs straight, try to touch the forehead to the knees. Suspend the breath for 3 seconds.

Posture 4: Ashwa Sanchalanasana—Equestrian Posture
Chant mantra: *'Om Bhanave Namaha'* (Salutation to He who illuminates).

- ► Keep both your hands fixed on the floor, inhaling extend your right leg backwards, as far as possible. Your right toes should touch the floor.
- ► Arch the spine, look upwards and balance the body.

Posture 5: Adhomukha Shvanasana—Downward Dog Posture
Chant mantra: *'Om Khagaye Namaha'* (Salutation to the All-pervading One).

- Exhaling, bring the left foot beside the right, simultaneously raise the hips and lower the head between the arms, so that the body forms an inverted V.
- Keeping the legs and arms straight, press the heels towards the floor and push the head lower. Sustain the posture for 3 seconds.

Posture 6: Ashtanga Namaskarasana—The Eight-limb Salutation
Chant mantra: '*Om Pushne Namaha*' (Salutation to the nourisher and giver of strength).

- Retaining the breath, bend and touch the knees to the floor. Bring the chest and chin to the floor keeping the hips elevated. Hold the posture for 3 seconds.
- The hands, chin, chest, knees and toes touch the floor and the spine is arched.

Posture 7: Urdhvamukha Shvanasana—Upward Dog Posture
Chant mantra: '*Om Hiranyagarbhaya Namaha*' (Salutation to the golden cosmic womb).

- Inhaling, lower your hips to the ground. Simultaneously straighten your arms and raise your head to look up and arch your back. Check that your legs, knees and toes remain together.
- Keep your arms and legs straight. Stay in this posture for 3 seconds retaining the breath.

Posture 8: Adhomukha Shvanasana—Downward Dog Posture

Chant mantra: '*Om Marichaye Namaha*' (Saluation to the golden rays of the Sun).

- While exhaling from the Bhujangasana position, raise the hips upwards and push the head downwards and inwards to form an inverted V, being careful that the heels touch the floor.
- Remain in the posture for 3 seconds suspending the breath.

Posture 9: Ashwa Sanchalanasana—Equestrian Posture

Chant mantra: 'Om Adityaye Namaha' (Salutation to the son of Aditi, the Cosmic Mother).

- ► Keeping both your hands fixed, inhaling bring your right leg forward, placing the foot near the inside of your right hand.
- ► Simultaneously, arch your spine, look up and keep your arms straight. Hold the position for 3 seconds retaining your breath.

Posture 10: Hastapadasana—Hands to Leg Posture

Chant mantra: *'Om Savitre Namaha'* (Salutation to the stimulating power of Sun).

- ► Exhaling, bring your left foot forward next to your right foot, straighten the legs keeping your hands fixed on the floor. Try to touch your forehead to your knee.
- ► Remain in this position, suspending the breath 3 seconds.

Posture 11: Talasana—Raised Arm Posture

Chant mantra: 'Om Arkaya Namaha' (Salutation to He who is worthy of praise).

- ► While inhaling, making sure that your head is held in between your arms, raise your arms and torso upwards.
- ► Remain in the posture for 3 seconds while retaining your breath.

Posture 12: Sthita Prarthanasana—Standing Prayer Posture

Chant mantra: '*Om Bhaskaraye Namaha*' (Salutation to the One who leads to enlightenment).

- ▶ While exhaling, in a sweeping arc bring your hands together in a namaste position at your chest.
- ▶ Remain in this position for 3 seconds.
- ▶ Repeat all the steps with your other leg to complete one round of Surya Namaskar.

Limitations / Contraindications

1. High blood pressure, cardiac problems
2. Vertigo
3. Abdominal inflammation
4. Sciatica, slipped disc
5. Menstruation, hernia, pregnancy
6. Any structural problems

Benefits

Physical

1. It influences the health of your entire body.
2. It stimulates and improves all your organs.
3. It strengthens your neck, shoulders, arms, wrists, fingers, back, stomach, waist, abdomen, intestines, thighs, knees, calves and ankles.
4. It invigorates your nervous system
5. It reduces redundant fat, especially the fat near the abdomen, hips, thighs, neck and chin.

Therapeutic

1. It alleviates various diseases linked to the digestive system and removes constipation.
2. It helps elimination of toxins.
3. It improves the vital capacity of your lungs.
4. It improves functioning of your endocrine system.
5. It improves the quality and circulation of blood.
6. It improves knock knees in walking.

7. It helps to cope with insomnia.
8. It helps regulate the menstrual cycle.

Psychological
1. Gives you poise, mental as well as physical.
2. It increases the power of concentration, optimism and self-confidence.
3. It increases emotional strength and spiritual growth.

Muscles Involved
1. Nearly all muscles and muscle groups
2. Mainly the vertebral muscles, cervical, thoracic, lumbar
3. Extensor and flexor muscles of the abdomen, lower extremities and arms

Names of Individual Surya Namaskar Asanas
1. Sthita Prarthanasana
2. Hasta Uttanasana
3. Hasta Padasana
4. Ashwa Sanchalanasana
5. Adhomukha Shvanasana
6. Ashtanga Namaskarasana
7. Urdvamukha Shvanasana
8. Adhomukha Shvanasana
9. Ashwa Sanchalanasana
10. Hasta Padasana
11. Talasana
12. Sthita Prarthanasana

The practice should be mastered by becoming familiar with each posture as each posture has its own limitations. Then the whole cycle of Surya Namaskara can be practised easily.

Number of Rounds
At The Yoga Institute we believe it is not the number of rounds that is important but the awareness of every muscle involved and the correct technique so that the relevant stretches are experienced and an attitude of reverence is generated.

Talasana—The Palm Tree Posture*

> *I lift myself up; committing not to*
> *be swayed by the tides of the world.*

The form of this asana and the movement involved is based on a palm tree. The immense flexibility without falling is the quality that needs to be developed within us, both physically as well as psychologically through the practice of this asana.

This posture stretches the muscles of the body. It has four variations.

Variation 1

Starting Position

1. Stand erect with your hands at your sides, shoulders relaxed but squared, chest lightly expanded and abdomen held firm but in normal contour. Keep your feet parallel to each other maintaining a one foot distance between them.
2. Avoid a forward or backward stance. Focus your eyes at one point straight ahead.

Steps

3. While inhaling, raise your right arm forwards and upwards towards the ceiling, simultaneously rising up on the toes in a synchronized manner.
4. Retain the position and hold your breath for six seconds.
5. The arm must be close to your ear in the final position. The other arm is straight but relaxed by the side. Ensure both your arms are straight but not stiff.

Posture Release

6. Turn your palm to face outwards and while exhaling, keeping your arm straight, bring it down through a backward and downward rotational movement. Simultaneously, lower the heels to assume the starting position.

Note: During completion of this movement, your hand must reach the side of your thigh and your feet must touch down at the same time.

Repeat the above steps with your left hand.

Variation 2

Maintain the same technique except instead of alternate hands raise both your hands together and bring them back down together in the same manner.

Variation 3

The same technique is followed except raise both your arms simultaneously from the sides, palms facing outwards and the posture culminates when the two palms meet overhead. Return to the starting position in the same way as mentioned earlier.

Variation 4

With the technique remaining the same, cross both your hands at the wrists in front of your body as a starting position. Then raise your crossed hands upwards, above your head while inhaling. Return in a similar manner as stated before.

Limitations / Contraindications
1. Spinal injury and abnormalities
2. Frozen shoulder and arthritis
3. Hypertension and serious cardiac complaints
4. Muscular and nervous agitation

Benefits

Physical
1. It facilitates maximum stretching of your body.
2. It enables free and natural accommodation of the internal organs.
3. Coordination of muscular activity is brought about by practice of this asana.
4. It tones the usually relaxed muscles of your abdomen.

Therapeutic
1. It develops the respiratory muscles and their vital index as there is an all-round expansion of the lungs due to the movements of the upper part of the body.
2. Flexibility of the spinal column improves and due to the stretch on the vertebral column, undue pressure on the vertebrae is released.
3. By stretching the ankle, shoulder joints, problems of stiffness arising from arthritis can be reduced.
4. It improves reflexes and neuromuscular coordination.
5. It tones the muscles of your legs and improves the venous function.
6. It improves the balancing capacity of the body and the gait.
7. It relieves sciatica pain and flat feet

Psychological
1. It helps to maintain a balanced state of mind.
2. It helps in remaining unaffected by the quirks of the world.

Muscles Involved
1. Planter flexors of the ankle, extensors of the vertebral column and the shoulder flexors

2. Hip abductor and abductors as stabilizers
3. Shoulder extensors are exercised while reversing

Yashtikasana—The Stick Posture*

I experience relief as I stretch, releasing my pent-up stress.

Yashti means a stick. Just as a stick on the ground is long and slender, this asana takes such a form. It stretches all the muscles of the body.

The all body stretch avoids undue strain as it is done in a supine position.

Method of Practice

Starting Position
1. Lie on your back on a mat with your legs fully extended, feet together and hands at the sides, palms facing down.

Steps
2. Inhaling, raise both your hands together above your head on the ground, stretching them.
3. Simultaneously, point your toes downwards away from the body as though the upper body is pulled upwards and the lower body downwards with the stomach stretched between.
4. Maintain the stretched position for six seconds, while retaining the breath.

Posture Release

5. Exhaling, relax your hands and toes, not returning to the starting position but retaining the hands above the head on the floor.
6. Repeat the stretching of your hands upwards and the toes downwards 4 to 5 times, taking a pause of three seconds in between each round if necessary.
7. After you have completed the stretching and relaxing as mentioned above for a couple of times, while exhaling, return to the starting position by bringing your hands to the sides of the thighs and relaxing your toes.

Limitations / Contraindications

1. Spinal injury
2. Frozen shoulder and arthritis
3. Recent surgery in the abdominal region

Benefits

Physical

1. It facilitates maximum stretching of your body.
2. It causes deep pressure on the muscular tissues as well as on the organs.
3. It tones the usually relaxed abdominal and pelvic muscles.
4. It provides adequate stretch to your spine.

Therapeutic

1. It aids better circulation of your blood.
2. The thoracic area opens up and hence improves your breathing.
3. It helps in correcting the faulty posture of rounded or drooping shoulders.
4. It is also good for those who have tennis elbow.
5. It eases the pain of joints.

Psychological

1. It is helps in de-stressing.
2. There is an overall relaxation to the body and mind.

Muscles Involved

1. Concentric contraction of gastrocnemius and soleus
2. Isometric contraction of the neck and the back
3. Anterior abdominal wall muscles are stretched

Hansaji J. Yogendra's Variations for Yashtikasana

Variation 1

1. Lie on your back on a mat with your legs fully extended, feet together and your hands at your side, palms facing down.
2. Inhaling, raise one hand above your head to rest on the ground simultaneously pointing the toes of the same side foot downwards.
3. Stay in this position, practising regular abdominal breathing for half to one minute, maintaining the stretch.
4. Relax the stretch and while exhaling, bring your hand back to your side and relax your toe.
5. Repeat with the other leg and toes.
6. Repeat the process using your opposite hand and leg.

Variation 2

1. In the same starting position as above, raise one hand above your head to rest it on the ground, stretching it.
2. Simultaneously, point your toes upwards towards the ceiling and towards the body so that you feel a stretch on the calf muscles and the back of the thigh.
3. Stay in this position, practising regular abdominal breathing for half to one minute, maintaining the stretch.
4. Relax the stretch and while exhaling, bring the hand back to your side and relax your toe.
5. Repeat with your other leg and toes.

Variation 3

This variation is same as Variation 2 except use both your hands and toes together.

*Parvatasana—The Mountain Posture***

Being steady and firm, strengthens both, my mind and body.

The mountain posture reflects the ideals of stability, steadfastness and resoluteness.

This posture has three variations to provide the spine with different kinds of stretches and movements (upwards, backwards, forward, sidewards and also a twist), all the while maintaining a firm base.

It also makes us aware of the importance of the faculty of sight, which needs to be focused, enabling us to maintain balance.

Note: In case you are practising more rounds, pause for a few seconds between each round.

In case you cannot sit on the floor, practise standing or sitting on a chair without arms.

Method of Practice

Starting Position
1. Sit erect in Padmasana or Sukhasana and keep your hands at their respective sides, palms facing upwards. Keep your head and neck straight and your abdomen tucked in gently, in normal contour.
2. Keep your eyes focused on a single point straight ahead.

3. Inhaling, raise both your arms together from the respective sides for an upward stretch, joining the palms to each other above the head.
4. Keep your arms close to the respective ears, your abdomen gently pulled inwards and back straight. Avoid bending your arms at the elbows and wrists, keeping them stretched and straight.
5. Fix your gaze fixed at a single point ahead.
6. Maintain this position for six seconds, retaining your breath.

Posture Release
7. While exhaling, turn your palm outwards, keeping your arms straight bring them down to the sides.

Variation 1

Starting Position
1. In the starting position as described above, raise both your arms together from the respective sides to join your palms above your head, keeping the arms straight, close to your ears.

Steps
2. While inhaling, bend to the right side keeping your hips firmly on the floor and your head tucked in between the arms. There should be no movement below the waist.
3. Immediately, exhaling, return to the centre.
4. Inhaling, bend towards the left side.
5. Immediately exhaling, return to the centre.
6. Turn the palms outwards and while exhaling, bring them down to the respective sides to touch the floor.

Variation 2

Starting Position

1. Follow the same steps till Step 3 of Variation 1.

Steps

2. While exhaling, twist your spine, pivoting towards the right side, maintaining fixity below the waist. This is an axial movement hence maintain the head, hands and upper torso as one unit while twisting.
3. Immediately return to the central position while inhaling.
4. Exhaling, twist towards your left side.
5. Inhaling, return to the central position.

Variation 3

Starting Position

1. Same as Variation 1.

Steps

2. Inhaling, bend backwards a little so that your spine arches backwards keeping the head locked in between your arms. Look upwards and backwards keeping the base fixed. Note that this does not involve too much of backward bending.
3. Now, immediately, exhaling, bend forward so that your upper body is parallel to the floor, keeping your head locked in between the arms moving as one unit. There will be a compression in your abdomen.
4. Maintain this forward stretched position suspending your breath for six seconds.
5. While inhaling, return to the centre.

6. As you exhale, bring your hands down to the sides.

    Note: You can perform the entire variations one after the other and once all the variations are complete return to the starting position with your hands down by the side.

Limitations / Contraindications
1. Arthritis of the knees and frozen shoulders.
2. Those who cannot sit on the ground can practise sitting on a straight-backed chair.
3. Hypertension and cardiac patients must not hold their breath and avoid variations.

Benefits

Physical
1. It stretches all your abdominal and pelvic muscles and loosens your hip joints.
2. It exercises your inactive waist zone, and helps reduce a flabby abdomen.

Therapeutic
1. It corrects minor postural defects of the spine and stretches the muscles of your back.
2. Unnatural curvature of the spine and minor displacements of the vertebrae are corrected.
3. Internal organs in your abdominal region get an internal massage; there is improved blood circulation.

Psychological
1. It improves your ability to stay focused.
2. It develops your strength, stability and longevity.
3. The mind gains deeper understanding of strength from the body.

Muscles Involved
1. Hip abductors, flexors and medial rotators
2. Extensors of the vertebral column
3. Shoulder flexors

Ardhamatsyendrasana—The Spinal Half-twist Posture**

Manoeuvring through the twists and turns of life
I become self-aware and self-reliant.

This asana is named after the great sage Matsyendranatha, the guru of Gorakshantha, who is considered to be the founder of the Hatha Yoga tradition. Though yoga practices are ancient and date back several thousand years, the tradition of Hatha Yoga seems to have gained a greater momentum after the sage Matsyendranatha.

This asana provides an excellent twist to the spine.

Method of Practice

Starting Position

1. Sit with both your legs stretched out in front and your hands placed on the respective knees or sides on the floor, maintaining an erect posture.

Steps

For twist on the right side

2. Fold your right leg inwards and press your heel against the perineum without allowing your knee to lift up.
3. Take your right leg, bending it at the knee, crossing it across your left thigh and place your right foot near the outside of the left thigh and bring your right knee close to your chest.
4. Bend the left leg at the knee inwards to place your foot close to your right hip.
5. Laterally twisting the torso on right side, let your left hand hold your right ankle/toe grasping the foot anywhere comfortable, in such a way that your right knee comes under your left armpit. Inhale.
6. Exhaling, give more twist to your spine and place your right hand across your back with the palm facing outwards.
7. Simultaneously turn your head and neck towards your right shoulder.
8. Suspend the breath for six seconds maintaining the posture.

Posture Release

9. Inhaling, untwist your torso, straighten your head and neck, bring your hands to the starting position, straighten your legs and prepare for practice on the opposite side.

For twist on the left side

Repeat the same steps as mentioned before but change the sides.

Note: This asana can be done both as a dynamic version as mentioned above or you can remain static in the position for a minute or two, alternating on each side, breathing normally.

Limitations/Contraindications

1. Hypertension and cardiac ailments
2. Hernia, pregnancy and peptic ulcers
3. Spinal injuries

Benefits

Physical
1. There is a lateral twisting of your spine.
2. The suspension of breath during the twisted position improves the venous blood flow in your abdominal region.
3. It tones and strengthens your abdominal muscles.
4. It opens the shoulders, neck and hips.
5. It increases flexibility of your hips and spine.
6. Deep and superficial muscles of your spine are massaged.
7. It tones the core muscles and also improves the health of your internal organs.

Therapeutic
1. It helps in management of diabetes, colitis and cervical spondylitis.
2. It relieves the spinal nerve from faulty habits of carriage.
3. It helps in curing lumbago and muscular rheumatism.
4. It is good for constipation and dyspepsia.
5. It improves digestive efficiency.
6. It helps in correcting curvature of the spine.
7. It helps in reducing respiratory problems like asthma.

Psychological
1. It increases concentration and alertness.
2. It improves mental efficiency and increases optimism.
3. It reduces mental fatigue while improving memory and concentration by improving the blood circulation in the brain.

Muscles Involved
1. Sternomastoid, anterior abdominal wall muscles, rotators of the vertebral column
2. Flexors of the knee, planter flexors of the ankle and medial rotators of the hip
3. Flexors and abductors of the shoulder, extensors of the wrists and elbows

Hansaji J. Yogendra's Variation of Ardhamatsyendrasana

Variation 1—Sitting

1. Sit with your legs outstretched and feet together.
2. Lift your right leg and place it on the outside but close to your opposite thigh, keeping your left leg straight.
3. While exhaling, twist your torso to the right as far as you can, look back, placing the right hand behind on the floor for support. Your left hand can rest comfortably on your right thigh.
4. Stay in the position for six seconds.
5. While inhaling, return to the centre and bring your right leg in the starting position.
6. Repeat on the opposite side.

Variation 2—Lying Down

1. Lie down on a mat with your feet together and hands at the sides stretched out at shoulder level on the floor.
2. Bending your left knee, place the foot next to the outside of the right knee. While exhaling, twist your hip, turning to the right to try to place your knee on the floor on the right side. Turn your head to the left.

In case you cannot touch the knee to the floor on the opposite side, go as far as you can.

3. Stay in this position for six seconds.
4. While inhaling, keeping your knee bent, return to the centre and stretch out your leg to resume the starting position. The head too returns to the normal position.
5. Repeat on the opposite side.

Bhujangasana—The Cobra Posture**

> *All potentials lie within; believing this,*
> *I rely on my inner strengths.*

The way the head is raised in the final position in this asana is similar to a fanned cobra and hence the name. The purpose of creating this posture is to imbibe the qualities observed in a cobra: determination, alertness and precision which are most desirable for a sadhaka on the path of yoga.

This is a backward-bending asana.

Method of Practice

Starting Position
1. Lie down on your stomach on a mat with your hands at the sides of your body.

Steps
2. Bending at the elbows, place your palms facing down near your chest, keeping your elbows close to your body.
3. Inhaling, raise your head and neck upwards to look up towards the ceiling. Raise your upper body only until the navel and not more. Make sure that your feet remain together and not get separated.
4. Remain in the final position holding your breath for six seconds.

Posture Release
5. Exhaling, bring your head, neck and torso down to rest on the mat.

1. Hypertension, heart ailments
2. Pregnancy, peptic ulcers, hernia
4. Hyperthyroid

Benefits

Physical
1. It tones up the deep muscles supporting the spinal column and trunk.
2. There is stimulation of the spinal nerves.
3. It massages and stimulates the adrenal gland.
4. It tones up the abdominal muscles.

Therapeutic
1. The alternative contraction and relaxation corrects minor displacement of vertebra.
2. It reduces constipation and flatulence.
3. It relieves generalized muscular pain.

Psychological
1. It helps develop faith and self-confidence.
2. It develops a calm state of mind.
3. It strengthens the willpower.

Muscles Involved
1. Sternomastoid and pectoralis major
2. Extensors of the vertebral column and neck extensors
3. Isometric contraction of the muscles of the upper limb

Hansaji J. Yogendra's Variation of Bhujangasana

Variation 1

1. Lie on your stomach with your legs together.
2. Your hands are placed palms facing down near your chest.
3. While inhaling, raise your entire torso off the floor, the head tilted backwards and look up. Your back will be arched and the

hands are straightened.

4. Remain in this position for six seconds.
5. While exhaling, return to the starting position.

Variation 2

1. Lie on your stomach with your legs together.
2. Your hands should be clenched behind.
3. While inhaling, raise your torso off the floor with your head tilted backwards and look up. Your back will be arched and the hands are straightened.
4. Remain in this position for six seconds.
5. While exhaling, return to the starting position.

Variation 3

1. Lie on your stomach with your legs slightly apart.
2. Place your hands on the floor as in the main posture.
3. While inhaling, raise your entire body off the floor.
4. Remain in this position for six seconds.
5. While exhaling, return to the starting position.

Dhanurvakrasana—The Bow Posture**

> *I become strong and yet remain flexible,*
> *in both body and mind.*

The final position of the asana resembles a bow (dhanusha). Flexibility coupled with sturdiness is experienced with the performance of this asana physiologically. It also increases mental strength and assertiveness.

Method of Practice

Starting Position
1. Lie down on your stomach on a mat with your hands by the side.

Steps
2. Bend your knees and fold your legs towards the back.
3. Grasp the ankles of your legs.
4. Inhaling, raise your head upwards and simultaneously pull your legs upwards, arching the spine, keeping both the legs together.
5. While retaining your breath, maintain the position for six seconds.

Posture Release
6. Exhaling, lower the legs and head. Release the grasp on your ankles and return to the starting posture.

Limitations / Contraindications

1. Hypertension, heart ailments
2. Pregnancy, hernia, peptic ulcers
3. Serious spinal ailments and arthritis

Benefits

Physical

1. It puts great pressure on your abdominal area as your entire body is balancing on the naval area.
2. Your entire spine is arched; it greatly enhances flexibility of your spine.
3. It opens up your chest, neck and shoulders.
4. It tones your leg and arm muscles.

Therapeutic

1. It improves blood circulation in the abdominal and reproductive organs.

2. It aids elimination through intra-abdominal pressure.
3. It provides relief from flatulence.
4. It provides relief in generalized muscular back pain.
5. It provides relief in ankylosing spondylitis.
6. It aids in controlling diabetes.
7. It realigns your back thereby improves your breathing processes.

Psychological
1. It improves concentration.
2. It is very useful for overcoming lethargy.
3. It is a good stress and fatigue buster.
4. It relaxes your mind and helps in conditions related to depression.

Muscles Involved
1. Extensors of the hip, elbow, wrist and neck
2. Extensors and abductors of the shoulder joint
3. Flexors of the fingers
4. Anterior trunk muscles, rectus abdominus, quadriceps, anterior abdominal wall muscles
5. Sternomastoid and pectoralis major

Hansaji J. Yogendra's Variation for Dhanurvakrasana

Variation 1

1. Lie on your stomach with your feet together.
2. While inhaling, raise your right leg from behind and grasp your toes/ankle with your right hand.
3. Simultaneously, bring your left hand in the front and raise it straight up as high as possible to create a balance.
4. While exhaling, release your leg and bring it down, simultaneously lower your hand and bring it to the side.
5. Repeat with the other leg and hand.

Variation 2

1. Same as above.
2. Separate the legs as much as you can but keep them straight.
3. Bend both your legs and grasp your toes/ankles from behind.
4. While inhaling, raise your legs and your upper body as much as you comfortably can.
5. While exhaling, release the grasp and lower your body, bringing your arms to rest beside your thighs.

*Ekpadasana—The One Leg Posture***

I resolve to remain equipoised as my goals are set high.

Achieving steadiness of body and mind is the primary aim of yoga. A steady body is home for health, vitality and efficiency. Neuromuscular coordination and concentration of mind enables this steadiness. There are yogic techniques with simple steps that harmonize the body and mind together. Ekpadasana is one such technique.

Method of Practice

Starting Position
1. Stand with your feet together and hands by your side.

Steps
2. Using your hands, lift your right leg laterally and press the sole of your foot against the left thigh as high as you can, the heel preferably close to the groin and toes pointing down. For those who cannot lift their legs so high, avoid placing the foot against the knees but rest the foot, wherever comfortable, against the thigh.
3. Balance your body weight on the right leg.
4. Once balance is achieved, join both your palms in a prayer pose. Breathe normally.
5. Maintain the pose for a few seconds. If your body sways or you tend to lose balance, try to fix your gaze at one point ahead.
6. Bring your leg down and repeat the same procedure with the opposite leg
7. Gradually increase the timing of remaining in the posture from a few seconds to one minute with each leg.

Posture Release
1. Release your hands and bring down your leg to stand with your feet together and hands at the sides.

Limitations/Contraindications
1. Severe arthritis, lower back pain, sciatica, slipped disc, vertigo.
2. Those with weak legs, lack of or very weak neuromuscular coordination may find it difficult to maintain the posture.

Benefits

Physical
1. It strengthens the muscles of legs and spine.
2. It improves your body balance, endurance and alertness.

Therapeutic
1. Isometric contraction strengthens your muscle more efficiently and also strengthens the bone it is attached to.
2. It stimulates many areas of your nervous system.

Psychological
1. It develops your sense of equilibrium.
2. It sharpens your awareness and concentration.
3. It keeps your mind in the present moment.
4. It calms the mind.

Muscles Involved
1. Flexors, abductors and external rotators of the hip and knee flexors of the hip that are bent
2. Flexors and extensors of the leg that are erect and gluteus muscles

Hansaji J. Yogendra's Variation for Ekapadasana

Method of Practice

1. Lie on your back with your feet together and hands at the sides.
2. Keeping your left leg straight bend the right knee laterally and place your heel near the groin or as high up as you can so that the entire heel of the right foot is placed firmly against the inner side of the left thigh.
3. Raise both your hands above the head to rest on the floor. Join your palms together.
4. Stay in this position for six seconds.
5. Release your hands and bring them to the sides and straighten your right leg.
6. Repeat with your left leg.

Garudasana—The Eagle Pose***

I become one-pointed to realize my potentials.

It is important to maintain alertness and flexibility, both of the body and mind.

Garudasana—the name characterizes strength, flexibility and agility of the body as well as alertness, one-pointedness and sharpness of the mind.

Suppleness and elasticity of the extremities (the arms and legs) result through the movement of the joints.

Garudasana or the eagle pose is an excellent asana which embodies twofold twists of the extremities at one go.

Method of Practice

Starting Position
1. Stand with feet together and hands at the sides.

Step 1

Practice of Wrapping of Legs
1. While exhaling, lift your left leg and wrap it around your right knee from the front and take it back from behind the right calf, locking the ankle of your right leg with your left foot.
2. Once the balance on one leg is secured, try to straighten your torso.
3. Maintain the position for six seconds with suspension of your breath or breathe normally if you cannot hold the breath.
4. Inhaling, unwrap your leg and come to the starting position.
5. Repeat the same procedure with the opposite legs.

Step 2

Practice of Wrapping Arms

1. While exhaling, extend the left arm with the elbow slightly bent. Place the right elbow on the inside of the right elbow. Now push the left arm outwards and leftwards trying to wrap the hands to join the palms of both hands.
2. Maintain the pose for six seconds with suspension of breath.
3. While inhaling, return to the starting position.
4. Repeat the same procedure with the opposite hands.
5. Practise this step for some time to gain efficiency before hands and legs can be practised together.

Final Posture

1. Practise both Steps 1 and 2 simultaneously.
2. Repeat the same process with the opposite legs and hands.

Limitations / Contraindications

1. Severe arthritis and problems with the extremities, tennis elbow, frozen shoulders.
2. People with cardiac problems, hypertension and vertigo can practise Hansaji J. Yogendra's lying down variation.

Benefits

Physical

1. It strengthens the muscles, tones the nerves and loosens the joints of your legs.
2. It stretches your hips, thighs, shoulders and upper back.
3. It improves muscle tone flexibility in your thighs.
4. It develops the balance of your body.

Therapeutic

1. It helps relieve sciatica and rheumatism in the legs and arms.
2. It develops balance.
3. It relieves stiffness in the shoulders

Psychological
1. It sharpens your awareness and concentration.
2. It keeps your mind alert.
3. It helps you to cultivate confidence.

Muscles Involved
1. Flexors, abductors and internal rotators of the hip
2. Planter flexors of the ankle, flexors of the elbow
3. Protractors of the shoulder girdle
4. Flexors, abductors and medial rotators of the shoulder

Hansaji J. Yogendra's Variation for Garudasana

Variation 1

1. Lie down on your back on a mat with your feet together and hands resting at the sides.
2. Follow the same steps as in the main standing variation but perform them all while lying down.

Variation 2

1. Once you have reached the final position in the above variation, breathe normally and hold the posture.
2. With your arms and legs in the above posture, roll over to the right while exhaling.
3. Remain there for six seconds, holding the breath.
4. While inhaling, return to the centre.
5. As you exhale, turn to the left.
6. Inhaling, return to the centre.

7. Exhaling, untwine the arms and legs and relax.

Note: This roll-over requires abdominal and back strength. Hence, if you have abdominal or back problems, it is recommended not to practise this variation.

*Halasana—The Plough Pose****

I imbibe the resilience of the plough that tills the fields to strengthen my body and will.

The final posture resembles a plough. It is an asana where the spine is inverted causing a strong compression at the throat and abdomen. When the attention during the practice is steadied, the mind becomes steady and strong. This is a fairly advanced technique requiring strength of the neck and shoulders.

Method of Practice

Starting Position
1. Lie on your back on a mat with both your legs together and hands at the sides.

Steps
2. While inhaling, raise both your legs together forming a right angle to the body. (You may bend the knees before you raise your legs in case it is difficult for you to raise them up straight and use your hands for support.)
3. While exhaling, lower your legs towards and beyond your head in a semi-circular arc to touch the toes to the floor.
   a. The hands remain in the starting position (however, you may use your hands, if need be, to support the hips as you raise yourself up and once the legs are in place bring your hands down to the starting position).
   b. The legs remain straight.
   c. You may clasp your hands in the final position.

4. Maintain the final posture, suspending your breath for six seconds.

Posture Release

5. Inhaling, in 3 seconds left the legs up and lower your hips (with the aid of your hands if required and bending the knees) and then bring back your legs gently to the starting supine position.

Limitations/Contraindications

1. Hypertension, cardiac ailments
2. Pregnancy, peptic ulcers
3. Respiratory disorders
4. Cervical spondylitis

Benefits

Physical
1. The spine is well-stretched.
2. No other asana is more effective for spinal health than this asana.
3. Your abdominal muscles get toned and abdominal organs get stimulated.

Therapeutic
1. It benefits the nervous and digestive system as well as the genital organs.
2. It improves occupational contours or other defects of carriage.
3. There is acceleration of circulation in the spinal region.
4. Steady improvement in the tone and activity of the internal organs is observed.

5. The stretching of the posterior muscles supporting the spine aids their pliancy and raises their tonicity.
6. It helps in relieving constipation, obesity, sexual debility, menstrual disorder and spinal rigidity.
7. It improves functioning of the thyroid, parathyroid and pituitary glands.
8. It reduces back pain, lumbago.

Psychological
1. It helps in reducing stress and fatigue.
2. It helps in remaining peaceful.
3. Besides having an overall good impact on the spine and other parts of body, it makes your mind alert.

Muscles Involved
1. Flexors, abductors and the internal rotators of the hip
2. Posterior aspect of the scapula and posterior lateral aspect of shoulder are stretched
3. Protractors of the shoulder, flexors, abductors and medial rotators of the shoulder
4. Flexors of the elbow are exercised

Hastapadangushthasana—The Hand-Toe Posture***

> *Difficulties persist, but I accept the challenges,*
> *become stronger and flexible.*

This asana is very direct in its name, suggesting a body formation including the hands, feet and toes. Since these extremities come together, it involves a great amount of stretching to the muscles surrounding the major hip joint. It also affects the waist and helps in flexibility and toning of the lateral muscles.

Variation 1

Starting Position
1. Stand with your feet together and hands at the sides. Inhale.

Steps

2. Exhaling, kick your right leg in the front as high as possible and grasp the toe with the same hand, keeping the knees straight. In case you cannot hold your toe, bend your knee of the right leg so as to grasp the toe with the right hand and stretch the leg out in front. Try to keep the leg straight but if not possible you may slightly bend the knees.

3. Stay in the position for six seconds.

Posture Release

4. While inhaling, release the grasp and bring your leg down.

5. Repeat with the left leg.

Variation 2

1. Follow Step 1 one as before and when the leg is outstretched swing it to the right.

2. Stay in the position for six seconds.

3. While inhaling, return to the centre, and releasing the grasp on your toes bring your leg down.

4. Repeat with the opposite leg.

Variation 3

1. Follow Step 1 of Variation 1.
2. While exhaling, bend your right knee a little to grasp the right toe with your left hand.
3. Lift your leg up towards your left side as high up as you can as the right hand swings out to the right side to maintain balance.
4. Hold the position for six seconds.
5. Inhaling, return to the centre and release the toes and bring your leg down.
6. Repeat on the other side.

In case you find it difficult to maintain balance while grasping the toes in the different variations, you can stand with your hands at the waist as you perform the different motions.

Limitations / Contraindications
1. Severe arthritis
2. Vertigo (for vertigo you can practise the supine variations given later)

Benefits

Physical
1. It strengthens your core and legs.
2. It improves your body balance.
3. It stretches your hamstrings and hips.
4. It strengthens your arms and back muscles.

Therapeutic
1. Your liver and kidneys are activated.
2. Your digestive and reproductive systems are stimulated.

3. Your digestion is improved.
4. It helps relieve menstrual disorders.

Psychological
1. It helps to induce a steady state of mind.
2. It improves the sense of body balance and weight management on one leg at a time.
3. It improves mental attentiveness.
4. It brings forth stillness in the midst of challenge.

Hansaji J. Yogendra's Variation of Hastapadangushthasana

Note: For all these postures do not bend your knees to reach the final position of holding or touching the toes. In case you cannot touch or hold your toes, go only as far as you can without bending the knees.

Do not practise this asana in bed or on a soft surface. It must be done on a mat on the floor. These are sitting and/or lying down practices.

The first five are sitting variations.

Variation 1

1. Sit with both your legs outstretched and close to each other, toes pointed upwards, hands resting on the thighs.
2. While exhaling, lean forward and grasp your left toe with your left hand and raise your left leg as far up as you can. Take support of the floor with your other hand to maintain balance.
3. Hold the position for six seconds.
4. While inhaling, release your toe and gently bring the leg down.
5. Repeat with the other leg.

Variation 2

1. Same as above.
2. While exhaling, lean forward and grasp your right toe with your right hand, lifting it up and swinging it to the right as far as you can go. Take support of the floor with your left hand so that your body remains facing front and balanced. Turn your head to face left.

3. Hold the position for six seconds.
4. While inhaling, bring your leg to the centre and set it down.
5. Repeat with the left leg.

   Note: In the first two variations, you can keep both your hands at the sides near the hips on the floor instead of grasping your toes. However, in this manner the body tends to lean backwards so take care to keep your body comfortably erect.

Variation 3

1. Same as before.
2. Same as Variation 2.
3. Contract your abdomen and while exhaling, lift your right leg about one to two feet off the floor, swing it to the right, bring it to the centre and inhaling, put it down. All these movements are done in one gentle continuous flow.
4. Repeat with the other leg.
   (Refer to the above picture.)

Variation 4

1. Lie on a mat with your feet together and hands at the sides.
2. While exhaling, lift your right foot by bending it at the knees and grasp the right toe.
3. Straighten your leg and hold the position for six seconds.

4. While inhaling, release the grasp and bring your hand and leg down gently.
5. Repeat with the other leg in the same way.

Variation 5

1. Same as Variation 4.
2. Bend both your knees and follow the same method as above.

Variation 6

1. Lie on your back with your hands outstretched at shoulder level on the floor.
2. While exhaling, lift your left leg straight off the floor and swing

it up and to the opposite side so that the right hand grasps the left toe.
3. Simultaneously, turn your head towards the left.
4. Inhaling, lift your leg, straighten your head and placing the leg down, return to the starting position
5. Repeat on the other side with your left leg.

Variation 7

In the similar starting position as above, sliding the right leg to the right side, hold your toes with your hands in the picture as shown.

*Hastapadasana—The Hands to Feet Posture***

In all humility, I yield unto the inner spirit and the cosmos which constantly guides me.

In ancient Indian scriptures, it is said that the entire universe lies within oneself. The mighty mountains, rivers, oceans and all things material are represented within the body. This is so because the external world and the body are made of the same five elements.

The uniqueness of this asana is to respect and value one's inner being, yield to its intuitiveness. This asana is replete with humility and acceptance of the self along with surrender to the universe. It represents a cycle of energy generated within the body and offered to the cosmos.

On the physical plane, this asana ensures flexibility and stability.

Method of Practice

Starting Position
1. Stand with your feet together and hands at the side.

Steps
2. While inhaling, raise both your hands from the front above your head.
3. While exhaling, bring the your hands down to touch your toes or grasp your ankles keeping your knees straight. Also, remember to keep your head and hands together as a unit as you bend down or rise up for maximum benefit.
4. Suspending your breath, keeping your knees straight, try to touch your forehead to the knees. Stay in the position for 6 seconds with suspended breath or stay in the position breathing normally for not more than 2 minutes.
5. While inhaling, raise your hands up above your head.

Posture Release

6. As you exhale, bring your hands down to the sides in a sweeping motion.

Limitations / Contraindications

1. Hypertension, cardiac ailments
2. Pregnancy, peptic ulcers, hernia
3. Cervical spondylitis and slipped disc
4. Serious eye disorders
5. Spinal abnormalities

Benefits

Physical

1. It results in extreme stretching of your posterior muscles.
2. It brings suppleness to your spine.
3. Intra-abdominal compression provides good circulation and massage to your abdomen and pelvic viscera.
4. It tones your abdominal wall and reduces unnecessary fat deposited in the abdominal area.
5. It induces clavicular breathing and aids proper ventilation of the uppermost part of the lungs.

Therapeutic

1. It has a beneficial effect on your back, hips and hamstring muscles.
2. It helps to stimulate the urogenital, digestive, nervous and endocrine systems.
3. It aids in blood circulation to your head.

Psychological

1. It improves your mind balance.
2. It brings in a sense of humility and gratitude.

Muscles Involved

1. Neck, shoulder joint and hip flexors
2. Wrist extensors

Hansaji J. Yogendra's Variation for Hastapadasana

Method of Practice

1. Stand with your feet together, hands at your sides.
2. While inhaling, raise both your hands up above your head. Keep your arms close to the ears as though you are holding the head with your arms. Palms should be facing outwards.
3. As you begin to exhale, contract your abdomen, twist your torso to the right and go down trying to touch the floor on the right. Check that your knees remain straight.
4. Inhaling, keep your head between your arms and rise up fully (remaining on the right) and then return to the centre.
5. While exhaling, repeat on the left side.
6. Exhaling, bring your hands down.

Konasana—The Angle Posture**

Kona means an angle. The body takes the form of an angle in this asana. In this posture there are three variations taking the body through different motions in angle formation.

In forming angles, your body is bent and twisted in ways which you do not do so in day-to-day activities. Most of the bending and twisting in Konasana is from the waist which results in streamlining the contours of your waist and abdomen. There is an internal massage of the organs of the stomach through compression.

There are three variations of this posture known as Konasana 1, Konasana 2 and Konasana 3 at The Yoga Institute.

Variation 1*

*Adjustments and compromises are two sides of the same coin,
inhibiting rigidity and stimulating
flexibility of the body and mind.*

Starting Position
1. Stand with your feet parallel and 2.5 feet to 3 feet apart. Keep your hands at the sides.
2. Turn your head to face the right.
3. Rest your left palm lightly on the waist, palm facing down (at a right angle to the body), the fingers in the front and thumb behind.

Steps
4. While inhaling, as you bend laterally from the waist to the right side let your right hand glide down as far as it can go, simultaneously your left hand at the waist slides up towards the armpit.
5. Maintain this posture as you hold your breath for six seconds checking that your body, arm and elbow are not tilting forwards or backwards. In this position, your gaze is fixed on the fingers of your right hand.

Posture Release
6. Exhaling, return to the starting position by letting your left hand glide down and bringing your body up to stand straight while your right hand glides to your waist to repeat the same process on the opposite side.
7. Let both your hands down to the side. Bring your feet together or leave them apart if you are practising more rounds of this asana or its variations.

Note: Keep your hips and legs fixed as you bend sidewards.

Variation 2*

To be like the blade of grass, bending if need be, but not too
much, recognizing the importance of my spiritual self.

Starting Position
1. Stand with your feet parallel and 2.5 feet to 3 feet apart. Keep
    your hands at the sides.

Steps
2. Raise your left hand straight up
    from the side, palm facing out, so
    that your arm is close to the ear, the
    right hand loosely hanging by your
    side.
3. Your face should look ahead.
4. While inhaling, bend from the waist
    laterally to the right as far as you
    can go without tilting to the front
    or back.

5. Maintain this position while holding your breath for six seconds.

Posture Release
6. While exhaling, return to the standing position and lower your
    left hand.
7. Repeat on the opposite side.
8. On completion of bending on both sides, let your hands hang
    loosely at the sides and bring your feet together or leave them
    apart if you are practising more rounds of this asana or its
    variations.

Variation 3***

I spread myself unto the universe, twisting and bending in the
melee, recognizing my potential to accomplish the goal.

This variation of the angle pose constitutes multiple actions. It involves lateral twisting and forward bending of your spine. It creates abdominal compression and an extension to the spine during the twisting and bending.

Starting Position
1. Stand with your feet, 2.5 feet distance apart, hands at your side, feet parallel to each other.

Steps
2. Raise both your hands from the front, palms facing upwards till the shoulder level.
3. Inhaling, spread your hands to the respective sides and turn the head to the right (the hands are still spread apart). Fix your gaze on the fingers of your right palm and follow the palm as it moves.
4. Exhaling, twist your upper body from the waist towards the left and bend down so that your right hand touches the left toe. The head is bent down. Your left hand swings straight upwards towards the ceiling
5. Twist your head and neck to take the gaze up to look at the left hand. Hold this position for six seconds with suspension of breath.
6. Now look down and again fix your gaze on the right palm.
7. Inhaling, bring your body up straight continuing to look at the right palm till you are standing straight. The hands are spread apart. Exhale.
8. Now turn your head to the left, practise all the steps on the opposite side.
9. Once you have come up, exhaling, bring your hands down to the respective sides. Relax by bringing your feet together.

Limitations / Contraindications
1. Hypertension, severe cardiac problems
2. Vertigo
3. Facet joint abnormalities, scoliosis, resolving and acute disc prolapse, osteoarthritic spinal problems
4. Hernia, abdominal surgeries

Benefits

Though each variation of Konasana has its own intrinsic benefits, all have multiple benefits on the following levels.

Physical

1. It stretches, massages and tones the lateral muscles of your waist.

2. Your shoulder and hamstring muscles get healthy stretches.
3. Intra-abdominal compression gives a good massage to your internal organs.
4. It improves your abdominal muscle tone.
5. It increases flexibility of your spine.

Therapeutic
1. There is a mild readjustment of the spine and strengthens a weak spine.
2. It is good for muscular pains of the cervical, shoulder and lumbar regions.
3. It is good for scoliosis.
4. It helps managing ankylosing spondylitis.

Psychological
1. The physical benefits have effects on your mind at a very subtle level.
2. It brings peace to your mind as your body is relaxed at the physical level.
3. It brings attention inwards creating awareness of the physical self.
4. It improves the synchronization between your mind and body.

Muscles Involved
1. Sternomastoid
2. Erector spinae
3. Serratus anterior and trapezius
4. Anterior shoulder and lateral trunk
5. Hip abductors and gluteus maximus

Hansaji J. Yogendra's Variations for Konasana

Sitting Variations: These include three variations.

Variation 1

Practice 1*
1. Sit erect in Sukhasana, keep your abdomen tucked in and both your hands on the floor beside your hips.

2. Raise your right hand up from the side and bring your arm close to the ears.
3. Inhaling, bend your torso to the left. Remain in the position for 6 seconds retaining your breath.
4. Exhaling, return to Position 1.
5. Repeat on the opposite side with the opposite hand.

Practice 2*
1. Follow till Step 2 as in the previous practice.
2. Inhale, as you stretch your hand upwards and exhaling twist your torso slightly to the left and bend to the left.
3. Inhaling, return to the centre.
4. Repeat on the opposite side with the opposite hand.

Practice 3*
1. Sitting erect with your legs apart and abdomen tucked in, clasp both your hands behind your head.
2. Inhale, and as you exhale, bend your torso to the right, contracting your abdomen.
3. Inhaling, return to the centre and exhaling bend on the opposite side.
4. Inhaling, return to the centre.
5. Repeat 3 to 5 times on both sides.

Variation 2***

1. Sit in Padmasana.
   Repeat all the above movements described in Practices 1, 2 and 3 sitting in Padmasana.

Variation 3*

1. Sit in Bhadrasana.
   Repeat all the above movements described in Practices 1, 2 and 3 sitting in Bhadrasasna.

Lying Down Variations: These include two variations.

Variation 1*

1. Lie on your back on a mat with your arms at the sides.
2. Raise both your hands, sliding them along the floor, till your arms are touching the ears straight above your head.
3. Bend your upper body along with the arms towards the right side as far as you can.
4. Now take your right leg, gliding it on the floor as far to the right as you can.
5. Let your left leg follow the right leg as closely as you can.
6. Check that your entire body is touching the ground. It would have formed a C-shaped curve.
7. Stay in this position for at least 30 seconds to a minute, pointing and flexing your toes alternately.

8. Slowly return to the centre and repeat on the opposite side.

Variation 2

1. Repeat Steps 1 to 4.
2. Slide your left leg in the opposite direction (to the right).
3. Stay in the position for thirty seconds to a minute.
4. Return to the centre and repeat on the opposite side.

*Matsyasana—The Fish Posture***

> *I swim through the waves of time, not depending on the*
> *external, but taking sustenance from strengths that lie within.*

This posture defines the qualities of a fish. Besides swimming, the
ability to float comes easily. It induces relaxation once you are settled
in the posture.

Variation 1***

Starting Position
1. Sit in Padmasana.

Steps
2. Inhaling, recline backwards, supporting your body with your arms and elbows and lie down.
3. Cradle your head with your hands.
4. Close the eyes.
5. Maintain the pose for six seconds retaining the breath or stay in the position breathing normally or practise abdominal breathing.

Posture Release
6. Unclasp your hands, exhaling and taking support of your hands come back to the sitting position.

Variation 2**

Starting Position
1. Lie down on a mat with your feet together and your hands at the sides.

Steps

1. With the aid of your hands bend your right knee and place your right foot facing upwards on the left thigh as high near the groin as you can.
2. Bend your left knee and cross your left foot over the right ankle to place it on the right thigh as high as you can near the groin.
3. You can encircle your head with your hands or place them on your abdomen.
4. Stay in this position breathing normally or practise abdominal breathing.

Posture Release

5. Release your hands and use them to release your feet to the starting position.

Limitations / Contraindications

1. All heart diseases
2. Peptic ulcers, hernia
3. Spinal injuries, back problems
4. Severe arthritis

Benefits

Physical

1. Stretching of abdominal and chest muscles gives internal massage to your respective organs.
2. It strengthens and tones the pelvic floor and sphincter muscles.

3. It stretches your hip flexors.

Therapeutic
1. Stretching of your neck muscles helps in regulation of the thyroid function and thymus gland, which in turn improves the metabolic and immune system.
2. It helps in relieving abdominal ailments like constipation, inflamed and bleeding piles.
3. It helps in relieving disorders of the pelvic organs, especially the reproductive organs and maintains the health of the reproductive organs and glands by improving the blood circulation in the area.
4. It reduces the chances of occurrence of vaginal prolapse and stress incontinence.

Psychological
1. A sense of well-being prevails and a feeling of calm and relaxation is experienced.
2. It relieves stress and irritation.
3. It creates strength, awareness and harmony.

Muscles Involved
1. Hip abductors
2. Flexors and medial rotators
3. Knee and shoulder joint and elbow flexors

Nataprarthanasna—The Kneeling Prayer Posture**

My body and mind in harmony,
I think, speak and act with awareness.

Nataprarthanasana requires complete neuromuscular coordination and synchronization of movements of the body. It is not spontaneous or natural hence it needs to be developed through practice. Absolute concentration is necessary.

Nataprarthanasana enables one to achieve harmony between the body and the mind. Avoid this practice if you have any problems with your knees.

Method of Practice

Starting Position

1. Stand erect with your feet together. Keep your hands in a prayer pose near your chest.
2. Focus your eyes at one point straight ahead. Inhale.

Steps

3. While exhaling, slowly kneel down, keeping your legs and knees together. Gently touch the knees on the ground and sit on the raised heels trying not to bring the knees down with a jerk.
4. Hold this position for six seconds while suspending your breath.

Posture Release

5. Inhaling, lift your knees off the floor and slowly rise up again to come to the starting standing position.

   Note: In case you are unable to stand up in this way you can release your hands and take support of the floor with them and slowly come up.

Limitations / Contraindications

1. In cardiac conditions, do not retain and suspend your breath.
2. Stiff joints and vertigo.
3. Moderate and severe arthritis of knees.
4. Acute deep vein thrombosis, sprained ankle and sciatica pain.

Benefits

Physical

1. It creates flexibility of your hip and knee joints.
2. The muscles of your legs are strengthened.
3. It enhances the balancing capacity of your body.
4. It is excellent for women's health.
5. It strengthens your lower back muscles.

Therapeutic

1. It helps relieve flat feet pain.
2. It helps maintain spinal curvature.

Psychological

1. It brings about a balanced state of mind.
2. It brings your mind in the present moment.
3. It brings about a sense of humility and gratitude.
4. It creates awareness and concentration

Muscles Involved

1. Quadriceps, soleus, gastrocnemius and intrinsic muscles of the foot
2. Extensors of the legs
3. Plantar flexors
4. Extensor group of muscles of the ankles and toes

Paryankasana—The Seat Posture***

My body feels good as I stretch and relax it at the same time.

The word paryanka refers to a bed or seat. There are a few asanas which are particularly beneficial for the needs of women like Matsyasana, Hastapadangushthasana and Nataprarthanasana. Paryankasana is one of them.

The benefits of this posture are best derived when the posture is maintained. Begin with remaining in the posture for a few seconds and gradually increase the duration to not more than two minutes.

Variation 1***

Starting Position
1. Sit in Vajrasana.
2. Spread your feet apart trying to keep your knees together.
3. Sit on a mat in the space created between your feet.

Steps
4. Inhaling, lean backwards with the aid of your elbows and forearms and lie supine.
5. Interlace your fingers and hold your hands over your abdomen.
6. Maintain the posture with normal rhythmic breathing till comfortable but not more than two minutes.

Posture Release
6. Exhaling, return to the starting position, taking the help of your elbows and forearms.

Variation 2*

Starting Position
1. Lie on a mat with your feet stretched out together and your hands at the sides.

Steps

2. Bend your right leg outwards at the knee and bring your heel as close to the hips/thighs as possible. Use your hands if necessary to place the foot next to the hip.
3. Do it similarly with your left leg.
4. Once the legs are in position, place your clasped hands on your abdomen and practise normal or abdominal breathing.
5. Take care not to lift or arch your back.

Posture Release

6. Release one leg at a time slowly to return to the starting position.

   Note: In case bending both your legs together is not easy or possible for you, practise with alternate legs, keeping your other leg straight.

Limitations / Contraindication

1. Moderate to severe arthritis
2. Pregnancy beyond fourth month

Benefits

Physical
1. It expands your lungs and chest.
2. It stretches your diaphragm and the abdominal organs.
3. It stretches the feet quadriceps.

Therapeutic
1. It helps with lymph drainage, as the lymph flows from the abdomen into the chest and supports lymph drainage under the collar bones.
2. It benefits the thyroid and parathyroid as your anterior neck spine is stretched and toned.
3. It is beneficial for kyphosis.
4. It improves your digestion.
5. It relieves menstrual pain.

Psychological
1. It relieves physical and mental stress.
2. It stills the mind.
3. It improves focus.

Muscles Involved
1. Extensors of the legs
2. Hamstring and quadriceps
3. Medial rotators of the hip
4. Plantar and knee flexors
5. Hip and elbow flexors

Pavanamuktasana—The Air Free Posture*

Not holding on to things, I 'let go' and feel relief,
both emotionally and physically.

Our body accumulates stresses of all kinds. When they are released there is a wave of peace and relaxation. This asana very simple to perform yet has plenty of benefits. The practice of this posture releases flatulence and helps relieve indigestion and constipation.

You can enjoy the benefits of this asana by performing either in the dynamic way or you can remain in the posture for one to two minutes breathing normally.

Note: For those with a weak abdomen, or not used to exercise are requested not to put pressure in the final position.

Variation 1—Ekapada (with one leg)

Starting Position
1. Lie supine at full length on a mat with your feet together and hands at the sides. Inhale.

Steps
2. Exhaling, raise your right leg, fold it at the knee joint and clasp your knee (or shin) with both your hands interlocking at the arms.
3. Pull the knee up to your chest and keep it firmly pressed suspending your breath and maintain the posture for six seconds.

Posture Release
4. Release your clasped hands, inhaling, straighten your leg and bring it to the starting position.
5. Repeat with the other leg.

Variation 2—Dvipada (with both the legs together)

The steps are the same as before except perform by lifting both the legs together.

Limitations / Contraindications

1. Abdominal surgery, inflammation, pain.
2. Cardiac ailments.
3. Hernia, piles.
4. Not recommended for women during menstruation and pregnancy.

Benefits

Physical

1. It stretches your lower back, hips and thighs.
2. The intra-abdominal compression provides good circulation and massage to your abdomen and pelvic viscera.
3. It stretches your arms, shoulders and neck.

Therapeutic

1. This posture gives relief to flatulence by quickening the movement and expulsion of the intestinal flatus.
2. A flabby abdomen, subnormal functions of the abdominal viscera and pelvic organs respond favourably to this posture.
3. There is a deep internal pressure massage and stretching of the network of muscles, ligaments and tendons of the waist zone and the pelvis.
4. It cures chronic constipation, sluggish liver, weak functioning of the abdominal and the pelvic organs.

Psychological

1. It alleviates mental sluggishness by enabling the release of toxins from the body.

2. It brings about mental clarity.

Muscles Involved
1. Hip, knee, finger flexors
2. Shoulder muscles, triceps, gluteus maximus and hamstrings

Hansaji J. Yogendra's Variations

Variation 1—Standing

1. Stand with your feet together and hands at the sides.
2. Lift your right leg, bending it at the knee and with both your hands press the knee on your abdomen.
3. Hold the position for a few seconds and bring your leg down.
4. Repeat with the other leg.

Variation 2—Sitting

1. Sit with both your legs outstretched and together.
2. Bend your right leg at the knee and press the knee on your stomach using both your hands.
3. Release your right leg and repeat with your left leg.
4. You can practise with both your legs drawn towards your stomach and clasp the knees with your arms.

Paschimottanasana—The Posterior Stretch**

Self-effort takes me to a point.
It is self-offering that makes me strong.

The word 'paschim' meaning west is used in the context of the posterior of the body and uttana for stretching. The need for spinal fitness is obvious. Exercising it in all possible ways is essential. Paschimottanasana builds up a strong and healthy spine, which in turn upholds the body. However, it is the intense abdominal compression that strengthens the core.

The process of practice of this asana and its final form brings about a sense of achievement devoid of ego and ushers humility.

You can perform this asana in a dynamic way as mentioned below or you can remain in the final posture for one to two minutes breathing normally.

Method of Practice

Starting Position

1. Sit on a mat with your legs fully stretched and your toes facing upwards.
2. Keep your spine, shoulders, neck erect and look straight ahead.
3. Keep your hands relaxed beside your body with your palms facing down.

Steps

4. While inhaling, lean backwards keeping both your hands beside your chest folded at the elbow, palms facing downwards. Your elbows should not jut out.
5. While exhaling, bend forward stretching your hands to hold the toes, trying to touch the head to the knees without bending your knees. At this stage, you can try to lower your elbows to touch the floor if possible.

Posture Release

6. Remain in the posture for six seconds while suspending your breath.

7. While inhaling, return to the starting position.

Caution: This final position is not easily attained. It is recommended that you try as much as you can and practise regularly. Overdoing this practice may cause injury.

Limitations/Contraindications
1. Hypertension, heart ailments
2. Pregnancy, peptic ulcers, hernia
3. Hyperthyroid
4. Serious spinal disorders
5. Myopia, glaucoma and serious eye disorders

Benefits

Physical
1. It brings about deep intra-abdominal compression and a massage

to your abdominal viscera.

2. It stretches the superficial and deep muscles of your ankles, legs and shoulders.

3. It stretches the spine and brings flexibility.

Therapeutic

4. Maximum posterior stretch to the spine helps in correcting minor deformities of the curvature of the spine and improves blood circulation in the veins and arteries.

5. It relieves constipation, weak digestion and improves a sluggish liver.

6. Abdominal compression helps reduce fat deposits in the abdomen.

Psychological

7. It acts as a stress reliever.

8. It calms your mind.

9. It enhances your concentration.

Muscles Involved

1. Ankle dorsi, knee, shoulder, finger and plantar flexors

2. Vertebral column, hip and knee extensors

3. Isometric contraction of forearm, arm, shoulder girdle

4. Abductor, medial rotators

Hansaji J. Yogendra's Variation for Paschimottanasana

Method of Practice

Steps 1 to 4 remain the same as in the main practice.

5. While exhaling, turn your torso to the right as far as possible, leaning forward, extending your hands straight and trying to touch the floor ahead on the right. Check that your left hip is not lifted.

6. Remain in the position for six seconds.

7. Inhaling, return to the centre.

8. While exhaling, repeat on the opposite side.

9. Inhaling, return to the centre.

10. Exhaling, lower hands and relax your hands on the thighs.

Ardha Sarvangasana—The Partial Shoulder Stand**

Achievement is not instantaneous, with consistent effort,
I progress gradually and steadily.

This posture is both a preparatory posture for Sarvangasana as well as for those who for some reason cannot practise Sarvangasana.

Method of Practice

Starting Position
1. Lie supine on a mat with your feet together and hands at the sides. Inhale.

Steps
2. Bend both your knees, feet close to the hips. Using your hands to lift the hips up, exhaling, raise the legs up together with both knees bent to make an angle with the body from the hips.
3. The chin is set in the jugular notch.
4. Maintain this pose for a few seconds or as long as convenient but not longer than two minutes, the breathing slow, rhythmic and natural.

Posture Release

5. Slowly lower your hips towards the mat, releasing your hands from the back, assuming the starting position.
6. Take a few deep breaths to compensate for the reactions of head-low hips' high posture.

Precautions To Be Taken during Performance of the Asana

1. Avoid any possible strain, and the period of exercise should be fixed at the minimum.
2. It is also advisable to attempt this posture first in parts, and complete the pose only after a few weeks of initial training.
3. What needs emphasis is the fact that this pose should never be attempted after any form of rigorous gymnastics because the abnormal rush of blood to the brain at this stage might do more harm than good.
4. Take care of your neck.
5. The limitations/contraindications, benefits and muscles involved are the same as in Sarvangasana.

Sarvangasana—The Shoulder Stand***

> *For a while, altering the flow of nature,*
> *I become alert and rejuvenated.*

The words 'sarva anga' denote the entire body. It is one of the very few postures that is advantageous for all the systems of the body, especially the head that houses the brain. This inverted posture maybe difficult for a beginner but as the practice becomes steady this posture can be practised daily.

This asana can be performed in the dynamic way as mentioned below or you can remain in the final posture for one to two minutes breathing normally.

Method of Practice

Starting Position

1. Lie supine on a mat with your feet together and hands at the sides. Inhale.

Steps

Method 1

1. Follow the same procedure as Ardha Sarvangasana and straighten your legs up vertically. Keep your entire body straight and point the toes towards the ceiling.

Method 2

1. While exhaling, raise your legs up together, toes to point towards the ceiling. The knees remain straight. Use your hands to support your body at the back as shown in the picture.
2. The chin is set in the jugular notch.
3. Maintain this pose for a few seconds or as long as convenient but not longer than two minutes, the breathing slow, rhythmic and natural.

Posture Release

1. Slowly bend your knees, then, as you inhale, lower your hips towards the mat, releasing your hands from back, assume the starting position.
2. Take a few deep breaths to compensate for the reactions of head low and hips high posture.

Precautions To Be Taken during Performance of This Asana

1. Avoid any possible strain, and the period of exercise should be fixed at the minimum.
2. It is also advisable to attempt this posture first in parts, and complete the pose only after a few weeks of initial training.
3. What needs emphasis is the fact that this pose should never be attempted after any form of rigorous gymnastics because the abnormal rush of blood to the brain at this stage might do more harm than good.
4. Take care of your neck.

Limitations / Contraindications
1. Hypertension, cardiac ailments
2. Pregnancy
4. Respiratory disorders
5. Cervical spondylosis, spinal problems, neck injuries or trauma
6. High myopia, glaucoma, serious eye disorders

Benefits

Physical
1. It strengthens your arms and shoulders.
2. It keeps your spine flexible.
3. It nourishes your brain with more blood.

Therapeutic
1. It improves the functioning of your thyroid, parathyroid and pituitary glands.
2. There are favourable changes in vasomotor ability due to the increased interchange of blood in the upper part of the body, especially the thorax, the neck and the head.
3. Relief from congestion, through the rapid drainage of venous blood, in the abdominal and pelvic regions.
4. There is a wholesome effect of gravity on the various organs of your body above the waist, including the vital endocrine glands.
5. It is helpful in constipation, dyspepsia, headache, giddiness, neurasthenia, functional disorders of the eye, the ear, the nose and the throat, general and sexual debility, and similar ailments.
6. No other asana is more effective for increase of blood flow towards your brain than this asana, besides having an overall impact on the body it makes your mind alert giving a feeling of self-confidence and self-reliance.
7. It helps in prevention and cure of varicose veins.

Psychological
1. It relieves stress as it calms your brain and nervous system.
2. It helps to balance the moods and calms your mind.
3. It increases your confidence.

Muscles Involved
1. Trunk flexors and wrist extensors
2. Flexors and extensors of the lower limbs
3. Extensors of the neck and erector spinae
4. Isometric contraction of the hip and knee

Shalabhasana—The Locust Posture**

> *I persevere, and with dedicated practice,*
> *speedily move towards my goals.*

The final position of this asana resembles a locust or a grasshopper. Their hind legs are increasingly stimulated and strong. The locust moves quickly. The same quality is to be built up in your body. The instrument of locomotion and the muscles related to locomotion are strengthened by the backward lifting of the legs.

You can perform this asana in a dynamic way as mentioned below or you can remain in the final posture for one to two minutes breathing normally.

Variation 1—Using Alternate Legs*

Starting Position
1. Lie on your stomach with your chin resting on a mat, your legs stretched out and your toes pointing outwards.
2. Your arms should rest beside your body with your palms facing down slightly pushed under your thighs.
3. Close your eyes and be at ease.

Steps
4. Inhale. While exhaling, raise your right leg straight up as high as you can without lifting your hips.
5. While raising your leg, keep your palms firmly tucked in their place.
6. Maintain the final position suspending your breath for six seconds.

Posture Release

7. Inhaling, bring your foot down to the starting position.
8. Repeat with your left leg.

Variation 2—Using Both the Legs Together**

1. Follow the same process as in Variation 1 except use both your legs together.

Limitations / Contraindications

1. Hypertension, heart ailments
2. Pregnancy and peptic ulcers

Benefits

Physical

1. It strengthens your wrists, hips, thighs, legs, lower abdomen and diaphragm.
2. It tones your back muscles and sciatic nerves.
3. It tones and balances the functioning of your liver and other abdominal organs.

Therapeutic

1. It helps relieve cervical spondylitis and spinal ailments.
2. It stimulates the appetite.
3. It provides relief in backache and mild sciatica.
4. It alleviates diseases of the stomach and bowels.

Psychological
1. It develops self-confidence.
2. It helps in relieving stress.
3. It calms the mind and body.

Muscles Involved
1. Extensors of the hip
2. Anterior trunk muscles, rectus abdominus, quadriceps, anterior abdominal wall muscles

Hansaji J. Yogendra's Variation for Shalabhasana

Method of Practice

1. Lie on your stomach with your hands tucked comfortably partially under your thighs.
2. While inhaling, lift your right leg off the ground about six inches and bend your knee towards the hips as you contract the hamstring muscles.
3. Exhaling, release your knee and bring down your leg.
4. Repeat with the left leg.
5. Repeat the whole process with both your legs contracting the hamstring muscles in the final position.

Variation 1

1. Starting position same as before.
2. Bend both your knees backwards, tighten the hamstring and raise your thighs up a little only.
3. Bring your legs down and relax.

Note: In these variations, the effort is not about how high you can lift but the contraction of the hamstring muscles.

Trikonasana—The Triangle Posture**

The spiritual triangle; may it be the source of
my self-awareness, energy and strength.

A triangle is the form used in several ancient fields of study and practice. It is used in temple architecture and extensively in Tantra meditation. The yogis used a triangular formation in the meditative postures as it is said that this formation brings in and unifies the forces of Nature.

However, within the dynamic postures this is one posture that allows a triangular formation to increase energy and strength.

Trikonasana is considered to be an excellent posture for suppleness and elasticity. It exercises the various normally unexercised muscles of the body through adjustments of the arms, the spine and the legs.

There are two versions of this practice: Yogendra Trikonasana and the general Trikonasana.

Yogendra Trikonasana—Method of Practice

Starting Position
1. Stand erect with your feet together and your arms at their sides.

Steps
2. Inhaling, raise both your hands in front to the shoulder level, eyes focused ahead.
3. While exhaling, bend forward from your waist keeping both your legs and the spine straight
4. Touch your toes with the tips of your fingers, keeping your arms straight.
5. The spine, head and the neck are kept horizontal, the abdomen drawn in, the eyes fixed on the tip of your nose.
6. Maintain this pose suspending your breath for six seconds.

Posture Release

7. Return to the original position, while inhaling.

    Note: Avoid jerky and hasty movements. In case the final posture in this asana is stressful or painful do not remain in the final position but immediately come up as this asana causes strain in the neck area.

Limitations / Contraindications

1. Hypertension, cardiac problems
2. Abdominal surgeries, hernia, severe piles
3. Pregnancy, peptic ulcers, cervical spondylitis, slipped disc

Benefits

Physical

1. Makes your spine supple.
2. Tones your abdominal walls and waist muscles.

Therapeutic

1. It aids the proper ventilation of the clavicle region of the lungs.
2. It aids in correcting faulty postural habits.
3. There is a beneficial effect on the back, hips and hamstring muscles.

Psychological

1. It improves the mind's balance.
2. It brings in a sense of humility and gratitude.

Muscles Involved

1. Neck and hip extensors
2. Hamstrings and extensors of the vertebral column

General Trikonasana—Method of Practice

Starting Position

1. Stand erect looking ahead, with your feet two and a half feet to three feet apart, parallel to each other.
2. Raise both your arms up from the respective sides, palms facing up.

Steps

3. Turn your right foot outwards.
4. Turn your head to look at the right palm and turn your right palm to face down.
5. Begin to bend towards your right laterally and allow your right hand to go as far down along the right leg as you can without tilting backwards or forwards. Your gaze follows the right hand.
6. In this position, twist your head to look up at the left hand, which is straight up towards the ceiling. Maintain the final position for 6 seconds for suspending the breath.
7. Keeping the gaze fixed on the left hand bring up your body to Point 2.
8. Turn your left palm to face downwards and the right palm facing upwards repeat the process of bending on the left side.
9. Once the bending on both sides is complete, bring your hands to the sides and relax your legs.

The limitations/contraindications remain the same as in Yogendra Trikonasana.

Ushtrasana—The Camel Posture**

The immense potential that lies within me, unravels.

The camel posture has great value both physiologically and psychologically. It aims to develop a stronger spine and a leaner body and relieves minor aches and pains of the back.

This asana helps remove complacency and builds a stronger emotional disposition, unravelling the potentials.

Method of Practice

Starting Position

1. Sit on the mat in a kneeling position with your toes and heels together. It is best to keep the knees together but you may keep your knees slightly apart for comfort and balance.

Steps

2. Gradually lean backwards, and take your arms behind.
3. Place your palms on the ground, with your fingers pointing backwards and the thumbs towards the toes. Keep your arms straight.
4. While inhaling, slowly lift your pelvis, waist and body both outwards and upwards.
5. Gently allow your neck and head to fall back.
6. Remain in this position for 6 seconds holding your breath.

Posture Release

7. Exhaling, relax your torso and slowly straighten your head and neck.
8. Release your palms and resume the kneeling position.

Limitations/Contraindications
1. Abdominal inflammation
2. Ulcers
3. Slipped disc

Benefits

Physical
1. It reduces fat on your thighs.
2. It opens up your hips, stretches deep hip flexors.
3. There is relative stretching of your upper thighs, abdomen, thorax, neck and facial muscles.
4. There is an inverted pressure on the vertebrae from the small of the back towards your shoulder and neck.

Therapeutic
1. It improves your posture.
2. It improves your respiration.
3. It relieves lower back pain.

Psychological
1. It develops self-confidence.
2. It relieves stress.
3. It calms the mind.

Muscles Involved
1. Quadriceps, anterior abdominal wall muscles
2. Sterno-mastoid and wrist extensors
3. Isometric contraction of the muscles of the upper limbs

Hansaji J. Yogendra's Variation for Ushtrasana

Variation 1

1. Sit as described for the main posture as before or if you cannot sit in the way shown sit in Vajrasana.
2. Lean backwards and rest your palms on the floor as described above.

3. Point your face up and while inhaling try to gently arch your back.
4. Exhaling, return to the starting position (see picture under Variation 2).

Variation 2

1. Follow the same steps till Point 2.
2. While inhaling, lift your right hand off the floor and raise it up towards the ceiling keeping it straight up taking care not to take it backwards. Simultaneously, point your face up as well as gently give an arch to the back.
3. Exhaling, release the arch and bring your hand down to touch the floor behind in a sweeping arc.
4. Repeat with the other hand.

Variation 3

1. In the same starting position, you can place your hands on your heels instead of the floor behind.
2. The entire process remains the same.

Utkatasana—The Upraised Posture**

> When my body moves in a coordinated rhythm,
> synchronization and mindfulness increases.

The name of this asana represents 'ut' (raised) and 'kati' (waist). This asana is to raise your waist by rising up on the heels, lowering the body down and again rising up.

Utkatasana enables great neuromuscular coordination. Awareness heightens and the ability of being focused while performing activities increases.

Method of Practice

Starting Position
1. Stand erect. Keep your hands at their respective sides.
2. Keep one-foot distance between both your feet, which are parallel to each other.
3. Focus your eyes at one point straight ahead.

Steps
4. While inhaling, with palms facing down, raise both your hands

parallel to each other, in front of the body, up to shoulder level.

5. Simultaneously raise your heels to stand on the toes.
6. Exhaling, lower your body to a squatting position till your thighs press against the calves.
7. Hold this squatting position suspending your breath for six seconds.

Posture Release
1. Inhaling, rise up again on your toes.
2. Take a pause on the toes, retaining your breath for six s econds.
3. Exhaling, lower your heels to the floor, bring the hands down and return to the starting position.

Limitations / Contraindications

1. Moderate and severe arthritis of knees, acute deep vein thrombosis, sprained ankle, stiff joints, vertigo and sciatica pains.
2. Do not retain your breath if you are suffering from any cardiac condition.

Benefits

Physical

1. Flexibility of your joints increases.
2. The muscles of your legs and pelvis are strengthened.
3. It enhances the balancing capacity of your body.
4. It engages your core muscles.

Therapeutic

1. With regular practice, you could lose weight, especially from your hips.
2. It helps in relieving joint and back pains.

Psychological

1. It develops steadiness of mind.
2. It increases focus.

3. Regular practice imparts a sense of balance in the body and great determination to the mind.

Muscles Involved
1. Quadriceps, gastrocnemius, soleus and intrinsic muscles of the foot
2. Abductors and flexors of the shoulder
3. Extensors of the legs, ankles and toes

Hansaji J. Yogendra's Variation for Utkatasana***

Variation 1

1. Stand with your legs together, heels together (you can adjust the distance of the heels slightly to maintain balance) and toes pointing outwards and sidewards.
2. While inhaling, raise your hands to the shoulder level from the front and simultaneously rise on your toes (but not too much).
3. Squat down so that your knees are spread wide apart as you exhale and your hands remain extended at the shoulder level.
4. Remain in this position for six seconds.
5. While inhaling, rise up so that you are on your toes.
6. Exhaling, lower your feet and hands.

Variation 2

1. There is no starting position.
2. While keeping your body supported on your toes, raise your heels together, keep your knees wide apart and remain in the position as long as comfortable but not more than a minute.

Vakrasana—The Curve Posture

I become self-aware and ever vigilant, especially during the
unexpected turns and twists of life.

'Vakra' means curve. This formation and the process of this asana are to curve the torso giving a twist to the spine.

It can be done sitting, standing or lying down. It is useful for those who have a desk job. The waist and the abdominal organs are exercised.

Sitting*

Starting Position

1. Sit on a mat with your legs fully stretched forward, toes pointing upwards and hands beside your body, palms resting on the mat.
2. Keep your back straight, neck and head in line.
3. Stretch both your hands forwards and raise them to the shoulder level. Keep your palms facing downwards. Inhale.

Steps

4. Exhaling, twist your spine towards the right as much as you can ensuring that your head, neck, shoulders, hands and the torso move as one unit maintaining the hands parallel to each other and keeping your lower body firmly fixed to the ground.
5. Immediately while inhaling, come to the centre.
6. Exhaling, twist towards your left side in the same manner.
7. Return to the centre while inhaling.

Posture Release
8. While exhaling, put your hands down to the sides of the thighs.

Limitations/Contraindications
1. Severe back pain
2. Abdominal inflammations, ulcers, hernia
3. Sciatica

Benefits

Physical
1. It relaxes the muscles of your back.
2. It strengthens the muscles of your lower back.
3. It exercises your abdominal muscles.

Therapeutic
1. Low back pain is alleviated.
2. Flab on the lateral side of the abdomen gets reduced.
3. It relieves stiffness of the vertebrae.

Psychological
1. It increases concentration.
2. It makes you alert and attentive.

Muscles Involved
1. Lateral rotators of the vertebral column
2. Flexors of the shoulder joints
3. Isometric contraction of the anterior abdominal wall

Hansaji J. Yogendra's Variation for Vakrasana

Variation 1

1. Stand with your feet about two to two and half feet apart.
2. While inhaling, raise your hands from the front to your shoulder level.
3. While exhaling, twist your torso to the right as far as you can, simultaneously taking the right hand as far behind as possible. The left hand bends at the elbow. Refer to the picture.

Take care not to raise your left foot during this extreme twist. Also take care not to turn your left hip or thigh.

4. Remain in the position for 6 seconds.
5. While inhaling, return to the centre.
6. Immediately as you exhale repeat on the left side.

Variation 2

1. Same as Point 1.
2. Raise your hands to the shoulder level and clasp your fingers.
3. Bend your torso putting your head between your arms and continue bending but keeping the body straight to form a right angle at the hip. Your hands will be stretched straight out.
4. Contract the abdomen and while exhaling turn your torso from the hip to the right.
5. Remain for six seconds.
6. While inhaling, return to the centre but do not rise up.
7. Immediately as you exhale repeat on the opposite side.
8. Inhaling, return to the centre, straighten up, release your hands and bring them to the sides.

Viparitkarni—The Inverted Posture**

> *Sometimes, going against the milieu,*
> *I develop a renewed perspective.*

According to the authorities on Hatha Yoga, this posture of inverted balance has been formulated particularly with the objective of bringing about inner harmony and union of the opposites such as the arterial and venous blood flow, the afferent and efferent nerve impulses, positive and negative counterparts of bioenergy and so on with the aid of gravitation.

Besides having an overall good impact on the body it makes the mind alert.

Method of Practice

Starting Position
1. Lie down on your back with your hands at the sides.

Steps
2. Exhaling, with the help of your hands slowly raise your legs up as shown in the picture. Hold your body with the hands at the back for support and maintain steadiness.
3. Breathing normally, maintain this pose from a few seconds to 2 minutes depending on your expertise and comfort level.

Posture Release

4. While inhaling, gently lower your hips using your hands for support and return to the starting position.

Limitations/Contraindications

1. Hypertension, cardiac ailments
2. Pregnancy
3. Respiratory disorders
4. Spinal disorders
5. High myopia, glaucoma, serious eye disorders

Benefits

Physical

1. It regulates your blood flow.
2. It stretches your neck, torso and legs.
3. It also relaxes your legs.

Therapeutic

1. There are favourable changes due to increased interchange of blood in the upper part of the body, especially the thorax, the neck and the head.
2. Relief from congestion, through the rapid drainage of venous blood in the abdominal and pelvic regions.
3. There are wholesome effects of gravity.
4. It benefits the various organs of the body above the waist, including the vital endocrine glands.
5. It is helpful in constipation, dyspepsia, headache, giddiness, neurasthenia, functional disorders of the eye, the ear, the nose and the throat, general and sexual debility, and similar ailments.

Psychological

1. It helps to soothe and calm the mind.

Muscles Involved

1. Trunk flexors and wrist extensors
2. Contraction of flexors and extensors of the vertebral column
3. Isometric contraction of hip and knee joints

4.   Erector spine and neck extensors

Chakrasana—The Wheel Posture***

As the wheel in constant motion,
I move ahead, breaking free from the past.

Chakrasana represents the wheel. The wheel is a primary invention in the world enabling endless functions. Its movement generates energy. It is the fundamental movement of time!

Chakrasana is performed in four phases. It is recommended you practise the steps before you can practise the entire four phases seamlessly. Then incorporate the breathing rhythms. You can also break up the practices and master each phase and its breathing rhythms. Later, practise them all together.

Note: The steps of this asana are slightly complicated. It is best to try all the steps and phases independently before you integrate the breathing rhythms.

Method of Practice

Starting Position
1.   Stand with your feet two-feet distance apart, and parallel to each other and your hands at the sides.

Steps—Phase I
1.   Clench your fists and while inhaling, raise your hands straight up from the front above the head. Your arms must be close to your ears. (This step and the second step must flow seamlessly.)
2.   Arch your back as much as possible and look up without tilting your hips and waist forward. The body below your waist remains fixed. (This step will have to be mastered before the breathing rhythm is incorporated.)

Steps—Phase II
1.   As you exhale, in a sweeping arc bring your hands and head down together towards the feet. (Refer to the picture.)
2.   Bring your head down as far towards the knees as possible.

Steps—Phase III
1. In a sweeping motion, take your arms behind your back as high up as you can take them.

Steps—Phase IV
1. Clasping your hands at the back, take your head further towards the knee, forming a full circle.

All the steps from Phases III to IV are as you exhale.

Posture Release
1. While inhaling, unclasp your hands, clench your fists and with your head still down, bring your hands down and holding the head in between your arms, raise your torso up to the Phase I position.
2. Bring your hands down as you exhale.

Limitations/Contraindications
1. High blood pressure
2. Cardiac problems
3. Hernia, piles
4. Abdominal inflammation
5. High myopia, glaucoma, serious eye disorders
6. Spinal injuries

Benefits

Physical
1. It strengthens the muscles of your chest and waist.
2. It develops the muscles of your back, neck, spine and shoulders.
3. It strengthens the core.
4. It exercises the anterior and posterior muscles of your body.

Therapeutic
1. It acts as the remedial and preventive measure in constipation.

Psychological
1. It improves the balance of your mind.
2. It brings in a sense of humility and gratitude.

Muscles Involved
1. Retraction of the scapula
2. Extensors, abductors and internal rotators of the shoulder
3. Posterior trunk muscles and the gluteus maximus

Hansaji J. Yogendra's Variation for Chakrasana

Method of Practice

1. Lie on your back on a mat.
2. Bend your knees keeping your legs together.
3. Take your hands above your head, bending at the elbows to place your palms flat on the ground a little away from the head.
4. Taking support of your hands (the body weight shifts to your hands) and as you inhale, lift the torso off the floor as high up as possible.
5. While exhaling, slowly lower your body.
6. Bring your hands to the starting position.

Yoga Mudra**

Vairagya: letting-go is as essential as the breath exhaled.

Yoga Mudra symbolizes yoga. It polarizes the opposites. It brings about humility in the presence of achievement. It is representative of grace and modesty within greatness. It is the emblem of great understanding and wisdom which knows the frailty of human nature and also its boundless potential.

Method of Practice

Starting Position
1. Sit in Padmasana or Sukhasana, clasp your hands behind the back, the right hand holding the wrist of the left hand. Keep your head, neck and torso comfortably erect.
2. Focus your gaze at one point ahead of you or close your eyes.

Steps
3. While exhaling, bend forward to touch your forehead to the ground.
4. Maintain the position, suspending your breath for six seconds.
5. While inhaling, raise your torso up to the sitting position.
6. While exhaling, bend your torso to the right to touch your forehead to your right knee.
7. While inhaling, rise up to the centre.
8. While exhaling, repeat on the left side and inhaling rise up and return to the centre.

Posture Release

9. Exhaling, release the hands and bring them to the front to rest them on the knees.

Note:
1. While bending forward to touch your forehead to the floor in front or the knees make sure that the hips do not rise and the lower body is firmly fixed to the ground.
2. In case you are unable to touch your forehead to the floor, let your knees go down as far as possible without the hips being lifted.
3. Check that your shoulders remain relaxed when the forehead touches the floor or the knees.

Note: You can practise this asana in a static way by remaining in the final position (the forehead touching the floor in front) for a minute or two.

Limitations / Contraindications

1. Hypertension, cardiac ailments
2. Hernia, abdominal surgery
2. Cervical and lumbar spondylitis
3. High myopia, glaucoma, serious eye disorders
4. Acute pain in the neck and back, stiffness of the back and joints

Benefits

Physical

1. There is stretching of almost all the posterior muscles of the trunk and the neck.
2. It improves the muscle tone.
3. Deep intra-abdominal compression favourably affects the viscera.

Therapeutic

1. The lateral stretch stimulates vital areas of the colon. Ascending and descending colon gets good pressure thereby alleviating constipation.
2. Acceleration of the venous flow from the sex organs has a favourable effect.

3. The compression of the diaphragm and the abdominal walls provides massage to the abdominal organs and is hence useful in gastric conditions.
4. It helps prevent sagging of the uterus and postnatal laxities.
5. Lumbar pain is alleviated.
6. Improves the overall health of the abdomen and pelvic organs due to good blood circulation and drainage.
7. There is a favourable effect in the management of ankylosing spondylitis.

Psychological
1. It helps to soothe and calm the mind.
2. It brings in a sense of humility and gratitude.

Muscles Involved
1. Extensors of the vertebral column
2. Hip abductors, flexors and medial rotators
3. Knee flexors
4. Shoulder girdle retractors

Bhadrasana—The Auspicious Posture*

Mind and body are nature's extraordinary gifts
for my spiritual growth.

The final posture is difficult to achieve by most people. Hence, though being a meditative posture, dynamic movements are involved. This posture boosts confidence and creates a feeling of achievement.

It is symbolic of auspiciousness and peace.

Starting Position
1. Sit erect with your legs outstretched and hands at the sides.

Steps
2. Bending both your knees bring the soles of both your feet together.
3. Use your hands to bring the soles of the feet as close to your body as possible.

4. Once your feet are closest to the body, keep holding it, trying to push the knees down to the floor. You can also use both your palms to gently push the knees downwards in case Step 3 is difficult.
5. Once your knees are as far down as possible hold the feet with your hands, close your eyes and breathing normally, watch your breath. Or, you can place your palms on your knees.

Posture Release
6. Gently opening the eyes release one leg at a time to return to starting position.

Note: Though this is a meditative posture, to provide flexibility to the hip and thigh joint, you can make butterfly movements, that is, push the knees up and down several times before you practise watching your breath.

Limitations / Contraindications
Severe arthritis and pain in the hip and knee joints.

Benefits

Physical
1. There is extreme stretching of both the superficial and deep muscles of your thighs.
2. It releases stiffness in your hip joint.
3. It strengthens the lower abdomen.
4. It improves flexibility of your legs.
5. Your pelvis and groin muscles are strengthened.

Therapeutic
1. It is helpful in lower back pain, piles and pregnancy.
2. There is better blood flow to the lower body.
3. When practised during pregnancy it aids in labour.

Psychological
1. It calms the mind.

Muscles Involved
1. Abductors, flexors, medial rotators of hips
2. Knee flexors
3. Stretches the superficial as well as the deep urogenital muscles

Hansaji J. Yogendra's Variations for Bhadrasana

Sitting Variation 1

1. Sit with your feet outstretched in front of you.
2. Bend your right leg at the knee inwards and bring it as close to the body as you can. Refer to the picture for placement of the foot.
3. Drag your left leg on the floor as far out leftwards as you can. Do not allow the legs to lift up.
4. Remain in this position for a minute.
5. Repeat with the opposite leg.

Lying Down Variation 2

1. Lying down as in Variation 1, bend both your legs inwards at the knees and join the soles of the feet.
2. With your hands, you can press your knees down towards the floor.

3.   Once in this position, interlock your fingers and put your hands on the stomach and practise normal breathing.

Gaumukhasana—The Cow Head Posture*

When I am composed and calm all actions flow effortlessly.

Gaumukhasana is most conducive to establish harmony and rhythm which is most suited for concentration. It balances the two sides of the body as generally we prefer either the left or the right side. It also provides a firm grounding.

Method of Practice

Starting Position
1.   Sit with your legs fully outstretched.

Steps
2.   Bend your left leg, bring it from under your right knee and place your heel near your right hip.
3.   Bend your right leg, bring it over your left knee and place your heel near the left hip.
4.   Raise your right hand straight up above your head, bend it at the elbow towards the back.
5.   Take your other hand backwards from below, bend it at the elbow to grasp the right hand, interlocking your fingers as shown in the picture.
6.   The head must remain straight and facing front.
7.   Stay in this position as long as you are comfortable but not more than a minute is necessary.
8.   Unclasp your fingers and come to the starting position.
9.   Repeat with the opposite leg and hand.

Limitations / Contraindications

1. Severe arthritis of the shoulder joints or frozen shoulders
2. Arthritis of the lower limbs

Benefits

Physical

1. It loosens all your joints.
2. It stretches your spine.
3. It improves blood flow to the pelvic region.
4. It stretches the hips, thighs, ankles, chest, shoulders, arms and wrists.

Therapeutic

1. It helps to relieve stiff shoulders.
2. It helps to reduce backaches.
3. It aids in treatment of sciatica.

Psychological

1. Regular practice reduces stress.
2. It develops calmness of mind.

Muscles Involved

1. Wrist extensors
2. Shoulder rotator cuff
3. Forearms, thigh abductors, groin stretch

RELAXATION POSTURES

To 'let go' everything, even for a while, and
self-offering unto the universe is liberating.

The word 'relax' is used so often and mechanically without realizing its great significance. To be able to relax is a technique as well as an art!

If we are predisposed to stress and worrying, relaxation cannot occur naturally. It has to be inculcated at various levels, gross and subtle.

When we learn to relax the body consciously, the mind becomes relaxed. These techniques in yoga, through conscious relaxation practices, usher relaxation for both the body and the mind.

There are no limitations or contraindications for these practices except the full benefit is experienced if you do not fall asleep during the practice. Remaining conscious and being aware as you relax is the key to experiencing complete relaxation.

All it takes is fifteen minutes to refresh and rejuvenate the self.

Makarasana—The Crocodile Posture*

To just be is an achievement.

Observing a crocodile, it appears as though it is constantly at rest unless it is stimulated. It is an effective technique to overcome physical or mental fatigue and calm an agitated mind.

Method of Practice

Starting Position
1. Lie down on your stomach making a pillow with your hands.
2. With your legs outstretched, keep your heels apart and the big toes touching each other.
3. Once in the position remain motionless, letting go of all the weight on the ground.

Steps

4. Close your eyes and breathe normally and rhythmically. Remain in this position for about five minutes.

Posture Release

5. Gently open your eyes.
6. Slowly turn on your right side for a few minutes before sitting up.

Limitations / Contraindications

1. Psychological disorder—depression
2. Cardiac conditions and pregnancy

Benefits

Physical

1. There is deep relaxation for your shoulders and spine.
2. It relaxes your body completely.
3. It rejuvenates your entire body and mind.
4. It helps to breathe slowly, efficiently and deeply.
5. It relieves the mind and body tension.

Therapeutic

1. It relieves muscular and nervous tension.
2. There is relief from headaches, fatigue and insomnia.
3. It reduces anxiety and calms the mind—releases stress and tension.
4. Conscious relaxation normalizes blood pressure, pulse rate and respiratory cycles.

Psychological

1. It improves concentration and focus.
2. It induces a meditative effect.
3. It turns the mind inwards, calming it and preventing anxiety.

Dhradhasana—The Firm Posture*

To remain unaffected, pure and peaceful is my aim.

It is an effective technique to experience the rest of prolonged deep sleep in a short period.

Method of Practice

Starting Position

1. Lie down with your legs stretched at full length, kept together in a relaxed manner.

Steps

2. Gently turn and lie on the right side of body.
3. Fold your right hand at the elbow, and rest your head on the right forearm.
4. Your legs must be straight, the left leg over the right. In case you find keeping the legs straight difficult, you can bend the knees a little for balance.
5. Close your eyes and breathe normally. Avoid any movement of the body.
6. Maintain this relaxed breathing.
7. Gently turn and lie on the left side in the same manner.

Variation

Lie on the side and bend the legs at the knee at right angle. Follow the above method.

Posture Release

8. Gently open your eyes and sit up slowly with the support of your hands.

Limitations / Contraindications
1. Psychological disorders, depression

Benefits

Physical
1. This posture favours ease of breathing.

Therapeutic
1. It aids digestion.
2. It relieves nocturnal emissions and stressful dreams.
3. There is relief from headaches, fatigue and insomnia.
4. Conscious relaxation normalizes the blood pressure, pulse rate and respiratory cycles.

Psychological
1. It quickly rejuvenates the body and mind.
2. It reduces anxiety and calms the mind—releases stress and tension.
3. It induces a meditative effect.

Shavasana—The Corpse Posture

Am at peace.

True relaxation would mean a complete resignation of the body to the laws of gravity, the mind to nature.

Whenever physical or mental fatigue is experienced, or the mind is agitated, the practice of Shavasana is recommended. The complete relaxation of the voluntary muscles at once transfers the energy to the involuntary parts. This transfer of energy by voluntary action and involuntary reaction produces the necessary equilibrium for the renewal of strength.

Partial Shavasana: Method of Practice

Starting Position
1. Lie down on your back. Extend your arms by the sides such

that they are not too far or too near the thighs. Keep your legs comfortably apart.

2. Once in this position, close your eyes and remain motionless throughout the practice.

Steps

1. Breathe rhythmically, subtly and slowly.
2. Avoiding any movement of the body mentally relax the sixteen vital zones (Marmasthanan) of the body, by paying attention to each part separately.

   i. Toes ii. Ankles iii. Knees iv. Thighs and simultaneously the hands and arms v. Groin area vi. Pelvis vii. Navel viii. Abdomen ix. Chest x. Neck xi. Lips xii. Tip of the nose xiii. Eyes xiv. Space between the eyebrows xv. Forehead xvi. Top of the head.
3. Maintain this relaxed state for about 10 to 15 minutes.

Posture Release

1. Gently open your eyes.
2. Slowly lie on the right side for a few minutes before sitting up.

Shavasana

Starting Position

1. Same as above.

Steps

1. Close your eyes and follow the normal rhythmic breathing.
2. Avoiding any movement of the body, consciously switch off all nervous stimuli.
3. Maintain this state for about 15 to 20 minutes.

Posture Release

1. Gently open your eyes.
2. Slowly lie on the right side for a few minutes before sitting up.

Limitations / Contraindications
1.   Psychological disorder—depression.

Benefits

Physical
1.   It relieves muscular and nervous tension.
2.   It stimulates blood circulation.

Therapeutic
1.   There is relief from headaches, fatigue and insomnia.
2.   It reduces anxiety and calms the mind—releases stress and tension.
3.   Conscious relaxation normalizes blood pressure, pulse rate and respiratory cycles.

Psychological
1.   It improves concentration and focus.
2.   Restorative benefits and invigorates the entire body and mind.
3.   It induces a meditative effect.

13

THE UNIQUE PRACTICES OF THE YOGA INSTITUTE

Nearly a hundred years ago, Yogendraji, the founder of The Yoga Institute, realized the need for simple but effective and profound ways to take yoga out from closed ashrams to the householders and the sincere seekers.

The potentials within can be attained through simplicity. The elaborate postures are really not necessary. They may boost the ego.

The highest spiritual realization can be accessible to all through the dedicated, sincere and intense practice of a few, easy but powerful techniques.

Yogendraji and Dr Jayadeva, over the years have created certain unique practices which have been immensely beneficial in multiple ways to all those who have practised them.

The technique of conditioning is also unique to The Yoga Institute and its practice is explained in the section on Meditative Asanas.

Some of the practices are mentioned hereunder.

Nishpanda Bhava*

The drama of the world continues.
I let it pass, be still and hold my own.

This is one of the most powerful techniques developed by Yogendraji to inculcate a spirit of vairagya, 'letting go'.

We traverse life holding onto all and sundry, from our material possessions to our thoughts, opinions, likes, dislikes, grudges, regrets and our insatiable desires.

This simple technique teaches us that life goes by just as the sounds around us. These sounds represent life, its events, situations and people who come and go. We understand that they persist, acknowledge them and allow ourselves to move on without regret, analysis and judgment.

Method of Practice

Starting Position
1. Sit on a mat leaning against a wall with your feet apart and outstretched. Do not slouch. Let your hips be close to the wall so that your spine remains naturally erect.
2. Your hands should rest on your thighs with your palms and fingers loose and facing upwards.

Steps
1. Close your eyes and passively observe the passing sounds as they come and fade away. Do not allow yourself to dwell on any sound but let it go as it fades away. Pick up on the next sound in the surrounding atmosphere.
2. If there are no sounds then you can focus on some light instrumental music but no words as words tend to develop emotions and reactions in the mind.
3. Do not get judgmental or be affected by any sound in any way.
4. Sit in this manner for 5 to 15 minutes.

Limitations / Contraindications
There are no limitations or contraindications for this practice. It can be done by all.

Benefits

1. This technique, when understood and practised in its true spirit elevates us from the mundane to the extraordinary.
2. It is excellent to develop vairagya bhava.
3. It creates a feeling of 'body forgetfulness', which helps the body to heal faster.
4. It is recommended in every sickness of body and mind and otherwise.

Reflection*

> *Every activity, howsoever mundane, is performed 'mindfully' and not mechanically, is my mantra.*

Since the time you are awake in the morning till you retire at night there is a ceaseless to and fro of countless actions. You remember several of these actions if they are important but so many of them are done mechanically such as brushing your teeth to showering or eating, talking, working, and so on.

At the end of the day if you have to sit and reflect on every action it becomes difficult to remember many of them and especially in order as most of them were done mechanically.

This practice makes you acutely aware of your actions. Becoming mindful of every little action is like watching over yourself. You become aware of what you do and how and when you do things.

This practice is ideally done at night before retiring to bed so that you can go over your actions performed through the day.

Method of Practice

Starting Position

1. Sit in Vajrasana. In case you are unable to sit in Vajrasana, choose any comfortable meditative posture. You can also sit comfortably erect on a chair.

Steps

1. Close your eyes and sequentially go over the details of the day

in as much detail as you can without dwelling on them, judging, analyzing or understanding them. This technique is like running a film through your head without any emotion involved. It is a factual recollection of the events of the day in chronological order.

Note: This process can take anywhere from 10 to 20 minutes. Any more time taken would mean, either you are extremely mindful and are recollecting every little detail of your activities or you are stuck in one or two events and have lost yourself in analyzing or judging them, resulting in some emotion surfacing. The first is commendable but only experts and long practice can result in this. The latter is definitely not recommended.

Limitations / Contraindications
There are no limitations or contraindications for this practice. It can be done by all.

Benefits
1. This practice will enable you to become aware of all actions. It prevents mechanical activities and helps you to become non-judgmental. It is an excellent method towards 'mindfulness'.
2. The technique allows better planning of each day, to figure out where you are going wrong and the areas where you can improve yourself.
3. It is a powerful memory training technique.

Yogendra Laya*

Being completely immersed in all that I do.

It is very difficult to be absorbed fully in anything to the extent of observing, knowing and understanding, realizing and becoming one with it. Laya is the practice of absorption such that we begin to observe that thing in its subtlest detail.

Method of Practice

Starting Position
1. Sit in a meditative posture of your choice.

Steps
2. Begin by bringing your attention and awareness on the breath and witness the process of inhalation and exhalation, breathing normally and naturally.
3. As you become comfortable watching the breath, bring your attention to your nostrils and focus on the area of the nostrils as the air enters and leaves.
4. Observe closely the friction of air as it strikes the nostrils during inhalation and exhalation. Also, observe the coolness of the in-breath and the warmth of the out-breath.
5. Continue observing the breath in this way for 10 to 15 minutes, getting absorbed in the breath.

Limitations / Contraindications

There are no limitations or contraindications for this practice. It can be done by all.

Benefits

1. It totally arrests the activity of the mind.
2. It releases anxiety and tensions.
3. It is an excellent form of meditation.

14

PRANAYAMAS

As the breath moves, so does the mind;
When one is steadied, the other too becomes steady.

HATHA YOGA PRADIPIKA 11.2

The breath is the channel between the body and the mind. Its subtlety, yet sensed presence, enables communication back and forth. It is the medium yogis used to tame and master the mischievous mind.

Pranayama forms the foundation to meditation.

Patanjali's *Yoga Sutras* on pranayama:

'*Tasmin sati śvāsa praśvāsayoho gati vichedah pranayamah*' II. 49

Thereafter (after practice of asanas), commences pranayama,
The break in the inhalation and exhalation is pranayama.

'*Bāhya abhyantara stambha vṛttih deśa kāla sankhyābhih paridṛṣṭah dīrgha sukṣmah*' II. 50

This break is when the breath is held outside, inside and its space, time, number, length and subtlety are observed.

'*Bāhya abhyantara viṣaya ākṣepi caturthah*' II. 51

The fourth (stage) is beyond holding [the breath] inside or outside.

214

PRANA: THE VITAL BREATH

Breath is associated with every living creature from birth until passing away. It is the vital breath. In Indian philosophical language it is called 'prana'. The ancient treatises talk about the universal life force, 'mukhya prana, which operates at the macro, universal level. The life breath at the micro level within each living being is 'gauna' prana. However, prana is not to be understood to be the same as the spirit or soul (called by different terms such as purusha or atman).

Sages of yore realized the immense cause and effect that arose through prana via the simple external process of breathing; inhalation (puraka), holding the breath (kumbhaka), exhalation (rechaka) and suspension (shunyaka) of breath.

Prana has multiple functions at the micro and cellular levels, apart from the external processes as above and are known as 'pancha prana' or 'pancha vayus'.

The pancha (five) are Udana, Prana, Samana, Apana and Vyana, each having their area of operation. However, the operations are not watertight compartments as they influence each other and operate in unity just as all the organs in the body having their respective individual functions are yet a part of the whole organism and work in harmony and affect each other.

The Pancha Prana

Udana vayu operates at the level of the throat, face and head. Its movement is upwards and influences thought; the cognitive, affective, conative and retentive faculties. Its element or tattva is light (teja).

Prana vayu is the chest area or the thoracic region influencing the respiratory system and the heart. Its movement is lateral and its element is air (vayu).

Samana vayu has a spiral movement and its region of operation is the abdominal area impacting the digestive and assimilative processes. Its base element is water (jala).

Apana vayu governs the excretory and generative organs. Its movement is downwards. The associated element is earth (prithvi).

Vyana vayu governs the nervous system and accordingly its field is the entire body. The element is ether (akasha). The circulation of all nutrients and energy is also a function of vyana.

PRANAYAMA

The ancient yogis, observing and experiencing the functions and effects of movements of air that is inhaled and exhaled at the atomic/cellular level, formulated certain breathing patterns to enable the individual to bring under his/her control and mastery an activity that is involuntary, autonomic, spontaneous and mostly unobserved.

Thus, for example, observing the breathing rhythms as fast-paced during certain stages of emotional upheavals, strenuous exercise or the slowing of breathing during periods of mental and physical relaxation they realized that if the existing mind and body states were to be improved, changed, transformed or brought under one's control the breath could be used as an effective tool.

Another area influenced by the breathing processes is the pathways or flows of energy (nadis) through the entire body as well as energy generation and storage systems (the chakras). There is no exact parallel physiological organ or physical system to comprehend these complex and subtle elucidations as the nadi and chakra systems do not in any way correspond to any physical apparatus/organ of the body.

There arose a whole system of breathing to manage the mind–body complex called pranayamas. Several ancient texts such as the *Shiva Samhita*, *Gheranda Samhita*, *Hatha Ratnavalli*, *Hatha Yoga Pradipika* and several others explain different methods.

In *Hatha Yoga Pradipika* it is said, 'As the breath moves so does the mind, when one is made steady the other is (inevitably) steadied.'

Pranayama is to manage the breath in such a way that the mind becomes steady, the darkness (clouds of ignorance) covering the mind is cleared and it becomes ready for meditation.

YOGENDRA PRANAYAMAS

The traditional pranayama techniques mentioned in Hatha Yoga texts require a specific environment, a different mindset and strict norms of living for gaining success. For a householder, such practices are not easy and may cause more harm than good. Also, it is extremely difficult to devote so much time and commitment towards these practices.

At the Yoga Institute, Yogendraji had termed prana as bioenergy. Nearly a hundred years ago, he was the first to modify the traditional pranayamas to suit the modern individual, living a full life. On understanding the complexity of these Hatha Yoga texts and the fast-paced life of today, he formulated easy and simple to follow techniques which are called Yogendra Pranayamas and are sequentially numbered from 1 to 9.

Yogendra Pranayama 1 is primarily to develop awareness of breathing and improving vital capacity through equalization of the duration of inhalation and exhalation.

Yogendra Pranayama 2, 3 and 4 are devised to target three groups of respiratory muscles to achieve bionic efficiency in the clavicular, thoracic and abdominal muscles and become aware of the vast coverage of the lung area.

Yogendra Pranayama 5, 6, 7 and 8 are meant for efficient management of the four stages of the respirational cycle: suspension, inhalation, retention and exhalation respectively.

Yogendra Pranayama 9 is to regulate air movement for specific purposes through the use of alternate nostrils while breathing.

These nine Yogendra Pranayamas include the following:

1. Equalization of breath
2. Intercostal breathing
3. Clavicular breathing
4. Diaphragmatic breathing
5. Shunyaka—suspension of breath (post-exhalation)
6. Puraka—prolonged inhalation

7. Kumbhaka—retention of breath
8. Rechaka—prolonged exhalation
9. Yogendra Anuloma Viloma—alternate nostril breathing

Yogendraji incorporated into these a system of counts where one count is equal to one second. A breathing pattern with counts for inhalation, retention, exhalation and suspension of breath was formed so that this breathing rhythm could be incorporated into the practice of the asanas too.

It is also advised to regularly observe one's normal breathing. To become aware which muscles are used, the coolness of the in-breath and the warmth of the air exhaled.

It is important to observe the expansion of lungs and the diaphragm at work during inhalation and the slight fall of the stomach during exhalation in normal breathing. One must also observe how the diaphragm pushes the abdomen out during inhalation when in a supine posture, especially while performing diaphragmatic breathing.

Pranayama aids in increasing concentration, promotes steadiness of mind and body and removes impurities, purifying the pathways of energy flows.

YOGENDRA BREATHING RHYTHM

Yogendraji had devised a simple breathing rhythm to be followed, especially during the practice of asanas.

A breathing rhythm of 3:6:3 would mean:

- Three counts/seconds of inhalation.
- Six counts/seconds of holding the breath.
- Three counts/seconds of exhalation.
- Most importantly, please remember that this a ratio.
- Thus you can use a ratio 2:4:2 or 3:6:3 or 4:8:4.

In this book, henceforth, along with each practice of yoga (including practice of asanas and several of the Sahaj Bhavasanas) wherever there is the mention of breathing rhythms of inhalation, retention, exhalation and suspension, it is recommended you follow the aforementioned ratio.

In certain asanas, the suspension of breath may be for a different duration. In such cases, it will be specified in the respective places.

Note: In case any practice, especially asanas, requires staying in a particular posture for a longer duration, you are required to switch to normal breathing and not to hold your breath beyond the prescribed counts.

Number of Rounds for Each Pranayama

Many of the traditional texts do not specify the duration of inhalation, retention, exhalation while some do give numbers. However, it is difficult to follow the traditional systems, as there are a lot of other complex rules to be followed too.

Thus to put a number on how many rounds you can practise each pranayama is not practical as each person has different capacities and purpose of practice. Some may wish to practise for health reasons while others for developing yoga skills, breath awareness and reasons stated in ancient yoga texts.

As a general rule or suggestion, it is recommended not to exceed thirty rounds of all the pranayama practices put together in one sitting at The Yoga Institute. Thus, being very subjective no number has been put alongside each pranayama.

On a day, you can practise pranayamas once or maybe twice. More than that is not necessary for normal active people.

General Benefits of Pranayamas

1. Creates mindfulness and breathing awareness
2. Calming effect on the brain thus there is clarity of thought
3. Increased efficiency levels and productivity
4. Enhances memory and concentration
5. Helps to balance and regulate emotions
6. Improves mind–body coordination
7. Reduces impulsive behaviour

8. Increases stamina and energy levels of both body and mind
9. Steadies the mind and body

The Yoga Institute pranayamas called Institutional Pranayamas are designed for householders, they usher jnana bhava as a predominant bhava and target awareness of both body and mind. However, Yogendra Pranayama 4 induces relaxation, letting go and vairagya bhava. Pranayamas also inculcate dharma and aishwarya bhava, as they represent self-discipline and increase confidence and positivity.

General Limitations / Contraindications

1. As such there are no limitations for these pranayamas if the instructions are followed under the guidance of a trained yoga teacher. In case of any limitation in respect to a particular pranayama, it is mentioned separately wherever required.
2. Avoid holding your breath in case of hypertension, cardiac and respiratory problems and depression.
3. Though pranayamas have numerous benefits but when incorrectly done without guidance or overdoing them may lead to insanity, schizophrenia and may aggravate depression. By increasing the ego it may cause personality defects. It could also affect natural sleep patterns. It could cause fatigue and listlessness.

Before Commencing the Practice of Pranayamas a Few Observances Are To Be Followed to Maximize Benefits

1. Practise after relaxation, post an asana session or if you are practising pranayamas on their own do a preliminary conditioning in Sukhasana as explained in the section on Meditative Asanas.
2. Practise with utmost concentration on every step of the pranayama.
3. Avoid jerky movements of the breath.
4. Not recommended for children below the age of twelve.
5. Make a habit of cleansing the air passages thoroughly through Jala Neti and Kapal Bhati.
6. Practise in a well-ventilated room depending on the place you

are in. The room should neither be too hot or cold.

7. During pranayama practice, unless otherwise suggested, the mouth must be closed. Even during an asana practice you must remember to inhale and exhale only through the nose unless specified otherwise for a particular practice.
8. Avoid tight and confining clothes. Wear breathable natural fabric.
9. Before commencing the breathing techniques it is best to stretch your body.
10. Quick and jerky breathing should be avoided.
11. People with a weak heart and hypertension should follow the yoga breathing very mildly, adhere to a minimum ratio and should avoid retention of breath completely.
12. Keep your spine erect and hold your abdomen in normal contour, unless otherwise specified.
13. Do not unduly strain any part of the body, including the facial muscles.
14. Pranayamas should be practised on an empty stomach or at least three hours after a heavy meal.

Note: In case of vertigo, epilepsy, cervical spondylitis, giddiness, imbalance or observing a ritualistic fast and so forth, practise the pranayamas sitting down and avoid holding your breath.

THE INSTITUTIONAL PRANAYAMAS—YOGENDRA PRANAYAMAS

From the following nine pranayamas the first three must be practised standing, but if you are unable to stand for any specific reason then practise them sitting.

If sitting, check that you sit either on the ground, in a comfortable meditative posture or on a chair with a straight back. As far as possible do not practise sitting in a bed unless you have some ailment and cannot sit on a chair. Keep your spine erect and abdomen in normal contour. Your shoulders must be relaxed but a little backwards for the chest to expand and contract comfortably during practice. Take care to avoid slouching.

Yogendra Pranayama 1—(Equalization of Breath) Equal Breathing*

*Harmony between my thoughts, words and
deeds forms the basis of all endeavours.*

Method of Practice

Starting Position

1. Stand (or sit as mentioned above with hands on the knees) erect with your feet about one-foot distance (shoulder width) apart, hands at the sides. Keep your shoulders relaxed.
2. Keep your gaze fixed on a point ahead of you or you may choose to keep your eyes closed if you are able to stand steady.

Steps

3. Begin inhaling and exhaling maintaining equal counts for both. For example, you can use a ratio of 3:3, 4:4 or 5:5 depending on your capacity/comfort. This makes one round. There is no retention or suspension of breath.
4. Continue inhaling and exhaling slowly and gently. Concentrate on this uninterrupted flow of breath maintaining the ratio.
5. Practise about 4-5 rounds of this.

Benefits

Therapeutic
There is a sedative effect on the nervous system.

Psychological
1. It creates quietude and inner harmony.
2. It improves concentration.
3. Mindfulness arises.

Yogendra Pranayama 2—Intercostal Breathing*

*I expand my horizons to learn,
experience and understand more.*

Method of Practice

Starting Position
1. Stand (or sit as mentioned above with your hands on your knees) erect with your feet about one-foot distance apart, hands at the sides. Keep your shoulders relaxed.
2. Keep your gaze fixed on a point ahead of you or you may choose to keep your eyes closed if you are able to stand steady.

Steps
3. Place your hands gently on the ribs as shown in the picture, fingers in the front facing each other and your thumbs behind.

4. As you inhale fully, your chest will expand laterally and during exhalation the chest contracts. The intercostal muscles expand and relax. Keep the count of inhalation and exhalation the same/equal using a comfortable ratio that suits you. There is no retention or suspension of the breath.
5. Be aware of using only the intercostal muscles and avoid the use of the clavicular or abdominal muscles.
6. Practise about 4-5 rounds of this.

Benefits

Therapeutic
1. There is better oxygenation and improvement of the vital capacity of the lungs.
2. There is exercise of the intercostal muscles.

Psychological

1. It creates quietude and inner harmony.
2. It has a calming effect on the nervous system.
3. It improves concentration.

Yogendra Pranayama 3—Clavicular Breathing*

There are hidden potentials within that I discover.

Method of Practice

Starting Position

1. Stand (or sit as mentioned above with your hands on your knees) erect with your feet about one foot distance apart, hands at the sides. Keep your shoulders relaxed.
2. Keep your gaze fixed on one point ahead of you or you may choose to keep your eyes closed if you are able to stand steady.

Steps

3. Place your hands on your shoulders with your fingers in the front and your thumbs behind your shoulder as shown in the picture. Keep your elbows out at the side for full chest and shoulder expansion.
4. As you inhale fully, using the clavicular muscles allow your shoulders to rise up and a little back.
5. Exhaling, bring back the shoulders to starting position. Keep the count of inhalation and exhalation the same, maintaining the ratio. There is no retention or suspension of breath.
6. Practise about 4-5 rounds.

Benefits

Therapeutic

1. It is excellent to oxygenate the areas of the lungs under the clavicle, which are generally not used much.

Psychological
1. The experience of air within the clavicular region increases awareness, mindfulness and concentration.

Yogendra Pranayama 4—Diaphragmatic Breathing*

I ignite the epicentre, the fire of creativity.

Method of Practice

Starting Position
1. Lie on your back, knees bent and feet close to your hips. The knees and feet should be close to each other.
2. Place one hand lightly on your navel, the other hand by your side.

Steps
3. Inhale slowly, gradually and fully so that your diaphragm pushes your abdomen out.
4. Exhaling, let the abdomen fall down.
5. Keep the count of inhalation and exhalation the same. Maintain your ratio. There is no retention or suspension of breath.
6. Practise continuously for about 5-10 rounds.

Benefits

Therapeutic
1. It is excellent for women during pregnancy, menstruation and PMS.
2. It improves digestive capacity.
3. There is a sedative effect on your nervous system. Its practice relaxes your entire body.

4. It improves the vital and tidal capacity of the lungs.
5. It impacts fat mobilization around the abdominal region and strengthens your abdominal organs.

Psychological
1. It leads to quietude and inner harmony.

Yogendra Pranayama 5—Shunyaka (Suspension of Breath, Post-exhalation)**

> *Maintaining a void, even for a while, from the ever challenging and demanding world is very important.*

Method of Practice

Starting Position
1. Sit erect preferably in either Padmasana or Sukhasana or in any meditative posture of your choice. Place your hands on your knees with your palms facing down.
2. Close your eyes or fix your gaze at one point ahead.

Steps
3. Inhale normally. When the inhalation is complete begin exhaling slowly and fully till you feel no more air remains within.
4. Pull your abdomen inwards and hold this position for five seconds without any movement in the body. The emphasis is on experiencing the emptiness post-exhalation. The mind is still.
5. Let your abdomen relax before you take the next breath in. You can breathe normally a couple of times between each round.
6. Practise 4-5 rounds of this.

Limitations / Contraindications
1. Hypertension, cardiac problems
2. Pregnancy, peptic and duodenal ulcers and other abdominal disorders or surgery
3. Lower back disorders and slipped disc

Benefits

Therapeutic
1. It strengthens a weak stomach and activates sluggish digestion and colon.
2. It corrects the inflated lungs.
3. It preserves elasticity of and tones the abdomen.

Psychological
1. It reduces distracting thoughts, calms the mind and improves focus.

Yogendra Pranayama 6—Puraka (Prolonged Inhalation)**

There is so much I learn and imbibe to go ahead in life.

Method of Practice

Starting Position
1. Sit erect preferably in either Padmasana or Sukhasana or in any meditative posture of your choice. Place your hands on your knees, palms facing down.
2. Close your eyes or fix your gaze at a point ahead.

Steps
3. After a short exhalation, begin a slow, long, unbroken and gradual process of inhalation filling your entire chest cavity till the diaphragm. Take care not to forcefully extend your stomach. The inhalation time can be from 5 to 10 seconds depending on your lung capacity. The emphasis is on prolonged inhalation.
4. Once the inhalation is complete, exhale normally and completely.

5. Take a few normal breaths before the next round.
6. Practise 4-5 rounds with pauses in between each round.

Limitations/Contraindications

1. Cardiac and hypertensive patients must take caution not to overexert.

Benefits

Therapeutic

1. It improves the lung capacity by stimulating the lung cellular structure.

Psychological

1. It improves focus.
2. It has a calming effect on the mind.

Yogendra Pranayama 7—Kumbhaka (Retention of Breath)**

Whatever I learn, I retain, reflect and practise.

Method of Practice

Starting Position

1. Sit erect preferably in either Padmasana or Sukhasana or in any meditative posture of your choice. Place your hands on the knees with palms facing down.
2. Close your eyes or fix your gaze at a point ahead.

Steps

3. After a short exhalation, begin inhaling slowly and gradually till you feel full. Make a mental note of the duration.

4. Hold your breath within for double the counts of the inhalation. For example, if you have taken four seconds to inhale you will be holding the breath for eight seconds. (Remember to hold within your capacity only and never overdo this practice as it may cause harm.) The emphasis is on the retention of breath post-inhalation.

5. Exhale normally.
6. Take a few normal breaths before the next round.
7. Practise 4-5 rounds with pauses in between each round.

Limitations/Contraindications
1. Hypertension and cardiac problems
2. Pregnancy, peptic and duodenal ulcers and other abdominal disorders or surgery
3. Lower back disorders and slipped disc

Benefits

Therapeutic
1. There is a favourable effect on the intra-thoracic and intra-pulmonary air pressures.
2. There is increase in the lung capacity.

Psychological
1. It develops a sense of control.
2. It improves focus.

Yogendra Pranayama 8—Rechaka (Prolonged Exhalation)*

Holding so much; thoughts, ideas, feelings, opinions and more, binds me. By letting go I free myself.

Method of Practice

Starting Position
1. Sit erect preferably in either Padmasana or Sukhasana or in any

meditative posture of your choice. Place your hands on your knees with your palms facing down.

2. Close your eyes or fix your gaze at a point ahead.

Steps

3. Inhale slowly and continuously for three seconds.
4. Retain your breath for six seconds.
5. Slowly, gradually and without jerks exhale continuously for twelve seconds. This process may be difficult at first and sometimes the air will be exhaled all at once, jerkily or quickly. With regular practice, this pranayama can be perfected. The emphasis is on prolonged exhalation.
6. Take a few normal breaths before the next round.
7. Practise 4-5 rounds with pauses in between each round.

Note: In case the ratio is uncomfortable, you can reduce it to 2:4:8.

Limitations / Contraindications

Hypertension and cardiac problems.

Benefits

Therapeutic

1. There is a favourable condition in the lungs for better oxygenation.
2. There is a larger volume of carbon dioxide expelled from the alveoli.
3. It improves functioning of the diaphragm.
4. There is a massage to the abdominal organs.
5. There is better ventilation due to prolonged exhalation.

Psychological
1. It reduces thoughts and improves concentration.
2. It develops the sense of 'letting go'.

Yogendra Pranayama 9—Yogendra Anuloma Viloma (Alternate Nostril Breathing)**

> *Being mindful and concentrated forms the foundation of my intellectual and spiritual ascent.*

Method of Practice

Yogendra Pranayama 9 is different from the regular Anuloma Viloma Pranayama. It has been specially designed to increase utmost concentration, awareness and alertness.

Starting Position
1. Sit erect preferably in either Padmasana or Sukhasana or in any meditative posture of your choice. Place your hands on the knees, palms facing down.
2. Close your eyes or fix your gaze at one point ahead (it is best to keep your eyes closed once you are comfortable with the practice).
3. Use your little finger or ring finger and thumb of your right hand to manipulate the closing and opening of your nostrils.

 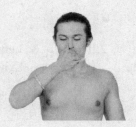

Ratio
The ratio used here is 2:4:2:2:4:2 2.
You can also use ratio 3:6:3:3:6:3: 3.

Ratio: 2(R I):4(H):2(L E):2(L I):4(H):2(R E) − 2 S)
      2(L I):4(H):2(R E):2(R I):4(H):2(L E) − 2 (S)

Abbreviations

R = Right
L = Left
I = Inhale
H = Hold breath
E = Exhale
S = Suspend breath

Steps

Refer to the diagram below for reference.

1. Close the left nostril with your ring or little finger (or both) and inhale for two seconds from the right nostril.
2. Hold your breath for four seconds by closing your right nostril (both nostrils will be closed at this stage).
3. Open your left nostril and exhale for two seconds.
4. Inhale immediately from the same nostril (left) for two seconds.
5. Hold your breath for four seconds by closing both the nostrils.
6. Open your right nostril and exhale for two seconds.
7. Close both your nostrils and suspend your breath for two seconds.

| 1. Right | 2. Hold | 3. Left |
| Inhale | | Exhale |

| 6. Right | 5. Hold | 4. Left |
| Exhale | | Inhale |

7. Suspend.
8. Repeat the entire process by opening your left nostril and begin by inhaling from the left and continue to complete one round.

Limitations / Contraindications
1. For people with hypertension, cardiac problems, pregnancy and general illness avoid holding or suspending the breath.

Benefits

Therapeutic
1. There is a tremendous increase in concentration.
2. It develops breath awareness.
3. It helps overcome psychosomatic problems, insomnia.
4. It activates the flow of breath in both the nostrils equally.
5. Its regular practice reduces blocked nasal passages due to a deviated septum.

Psychological
1. It arrests the thought process as your mind is completely focused on the activity of breathing.

OTHER PRANAYAMAS

These pranayamas are traditional. Considering the wide scope of readership of this book, the pranayamas that follow have been simplified to suit the modern yoga practitioner.

The traditional pranayamas are called kumbhaka and are advanced practices. These are best learnt under the guidance of an expert yoga teacher, hence the traditional instructions have been avoided. These have been presented in a simplified manner.

Shitali—The Cooling Breath*

Any thoughts I think, decisions I make, actions I perform, are best done in an equipoised state of mind.

Method of Practice

Starting Position

1. Sit comfortably in any meditative posture, preferably Padmasana or Sukhasana.

Steps

1. Pout your lips and stick out your tongue. Curl it so that the sides turn up and a hollow tube is formed in the centre.
2. Inhale slowly, smoothly and fully through the tube formed by the tongue.
3. Withdraw the tongue inside and close your mouth. Exhale through your nose.
4. Repeat it 4-5 times.

Limitations/Contraindications

There are no limitations. This pranayama can be practised by all.

Benefits

Therapeutic

1. It helps to reduce hunger, thirst and fever according to traditional yoga texts.
2. It helps in psychosomatic ailments.
3. It helps in reducing ailments of the abdomen.

Psychological
1. It develops calmness of the mind.

Seetkari—The Hissing Sound Breath*

A charismatic persona I develop, through a simple act.

This ancient pranayama is named after the sound it produces, as of 'hissing' 'seeeee...'

Method of Practice

Starting Position
1. Sit comfortably in any meditative posture, preferably Padmasana or Sukhasana.

Steps
1. Close your lips lightly and inhale deeply through your clenched teeth, creating a hissing sound. You may keep your lips partially open if you wish.
2. A coolness will be felt in your mouth and if the inhalation is longer it will be experienced all along till the stomach.
3. Keeping your mouth closed exhale through your nose.

Limitations / Contraindications
There are no limitations. This pranayama can be practised by all.

Benefits

Therapeutic
1. *Hatha Yoga Pradipika* says that through the practice of this pranayama one becomes like Kamadeva, the god of love. It is excellent for a glowing complexion.

The text also says that this practice enables reduction of excess appetite and thirst, excessive sleep and lethargy.

Psychological
1. It calms the mind.
2. It reduces emotional excitation and mental tension.
3. It is best for depression.

Ujjayi—The Victorious Breath*

Victory be mine as I practise with dedication.

From the word, 'jaya' originates ujjayi. It represents victory.

An important effect of this pranayama is its impact on the voice. Speech is considered very important in ancient Indian scriptures and yoga. Speech is a symbol of knowledge. It is divine. It is a form of expression of the innermost thoughts and knowledge. According to the oral traditions, learning is spread through speech.

The practice of this pranayama affects the throat region, resulting in benefitting the thyroid gland.

Method of Practice

Starting Position
1. Sit comfortably in any meditative posture, preferably Padmasana or Sukhasana. Close your eyes. The ancient yoga texts say this pranayama can be done standing, sitting or moving.

Steps
1. Keeping your mouth closed, constrict your throat and inhale through your nose making a sound from the throat. There will be effort visible at the throat. Continue to inhale till fullness is

experienced. Retain the air for six seconds.

2. Exhale through your nose with or without any sound and effort.

Limitations/Contraindications

There are no limitations. This pranayama can be practised by all.

Benefits

Therapeutic

1. There is enrichment of the voice.
2. There is stimulation and balancing of the thyroid gland.
3. There is nourishment of the dhatus, the vital components within the body.
4. The nadis (subtle 'flows'/channels of energy) are purified.

Psychological

1. It increases your focus.
2. It creates a positive attitude.
3. It increases the concentration power.

Bhramari—The Sound of the Humming Bee*

The cosmic sound reverberates in every cell of my body.

The resounding echo of the sound made by a humming bee is replicated in the practice of this pranayama. The humming sound is beyond language or phonetics. It resonates in the head region and in turn its resonance radiates and reverberates in every cell of the body.

The spiritual aim of this practice is to be able to listen to the sounds generated within the body. It is to be able to understand the great outside is manifested within. Practised daily, a calm and meditative state is created.

Method of Practice

Starting Position
1. Sit comfortably in any meditative posture, preferably Padmasana or Sukhasana.

Steps
2. Keep your mouth closed throughout the practice.
3. Inhale. While exhaling, make a sound of the humming bee slowly, smoothly and continuously in a controlled manner.
4. The sound need not be very loud but should create the vibrations.

Note: You may close your ears gently with your forefingers during the practice.

5. Repeat for 4-5 times.

Note: This is a prolonged exhalation and the sound must be during the whole period of exhalation.

Limitations / Contraindications
There are no limitations. This pranayama can be practised by all.

Benefits

Therapeutic
1. It gives relief when you are feeling hot or have a slight headache.

Psychological
1. It creates a peaceful atmosphere thereby reducing stress.
2. A meditative ambience is created.

Bhastrika—The Bellows Movement**

> *To be rejuvenated, all impurities and*
> *inertness must be removed.*

This pranayama is performed with robustness. 'Bhastrika' means bellows. It represents the actions of a blacksmith hitting metal with full force. Just like fire is necessary to shape and purify the metal, in this pranayama the forceful inhalation and exhalation produces heat for purification and energizing the body. This action helps in increasing lung capacity, purifying the lungs and strengthening the core.

Method of Practice

Starting Position
1. Sit comfortably in any meditative posture, preferably Padmasana or Sukhasana.

Steps
1. Inhale and exhale deeply and fully using the diaphragmatic muscles with vigour. The abdomen will be pulled in during exhalation and expand during inhalation.

A strong nasal sound will accompany such breathing. The process should be rhythmic and controlled, maintaining the speed as per capacity.

2. Practise about ten breath cycles per round. Relax for a few seconds. Practise another round. Practise not more than three such rounds in one sitting.

Note:
1. Practise this on an empty stomach.
2. If you are a beginner and not used to this pranayama, practise the synchronized movement of the abdomen and the breath before you begin more rounds of this practice.

Limitations / Contraindications
1. Hypertension, cardiac ailments
2. Abdominal disorders
3. Spinal abnormalities, pregnancy

Benefits

Therapeutic
1. It energizes the entire body and the mind.
2. It strengthens and tones the abdominal region.

3. It increases the vital lung capacity.

Psychological
1. It calms the mind.

Surya Bhedan

May the energies of the vibrant Sun be aroused within.

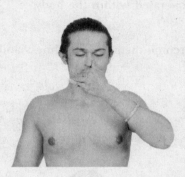

Surya means the Sun and it represents heat. It is associated with the right nostril. The word 'bheda' means to pierce. In this context, it refers to 'awaken' or arouse a certain experience or quality.

Method of Practice

Starting Position
1. It in any meditative posture of your choice.

Steps
2. Using the same hand mudra as in Yogendra Anuloma Viloma, begin by closing the left nostril and inhaling slowly, gradually, rhythmically and fully through the right nostril.
3. When feeling a fullness in the lungs, close both nostrils momentarily so as not to let the air escape from both nostrils. Immediately open the left nostril and exhale gently and fully.
4. Repeat the process once or twice.

Limitations and Contraindications

1. Avoid this pranayama in summer months
2. It is not recommended for high blood pressure and cardiac patients.

Benefits

Physical and therapeutic
There is warmth generated within the body.

Psychological

1. It helps to overcome mental sluggishness and laziness.
2. It is energizing.

Chandra Bhedan

Let the coolness and quietude of the Moon
envelope my entire being.

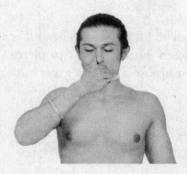

This pranayama brings a refreshing coolness in the body. It is excellent to calm a restless mind. The left nostril is associated with the Moon.

Method of Practice

Starting Position

1. Sit in any meditative posture of your choice.

Steps

2. Using the same hand mudra as in Yogendra Anuloma Viloma,

begin by closing the right nostril and inhaling slowly, gradually, rhythmically and fully through the left nostril.

3. When feeling a fullness in the lungs, close both nostrils momentarily so as not to let the air escape from them. Immediately open the right nostril and exhale gently and fully.

4. Repeat the process once or twice.

Limitations / Contraindications

1. Avoid this pranayama in winter or cool months.
2. Avoid it during nasal infections, coughs and colds.

Benefits

Physical and Therapeutic

1. There is a peace generated within the body.
2. It regulates the flow of bile.

Psychological

1. Mental restlessness is overcome.
2. It induces calmness.

15

KRIYAS

The purified and strengthened body, through the practice of
kriyas, becomes ready for further intense yoga sadhana.

KRIYAS

The traditional yoga texts such as *Hatha Yoga Pradipika, Gheranda Samhita* and others mention the 'shat karma kriyas', the six practices of purification of the body using different mediums such as air, water, heat and sometimes other means too.

Purification of the body is extremely important as it results in the unrestricted flow of energy throughout the body. Kriyas help the body to clear the energy pathways, alleviate various infections, toxins, several ailments and strengthens the immune system. They help to improve the functioning of the organs or body parts.

At The Yoga Institute, kriyas are considered as practices that develop aishvarya bhava, those that boost self-confidence and promote vibrant health.

In this book, the kriyas that have been explained are those which every yoga practitioner can include in their daily lives.

The complex kriyas have been excluded as they require direct training under an expert yoga teacher.

Neti—Nasal Purification*

A simple practice of self-reliance,
opens the pathways of well-being.

In Hatha Yoga texts the emphasis is on sutra neti (neti means using a cotton thread). Nowadays, we do not follow the custom of using cotton thread; a rubber catheter is used instead. This practice needs direct training under an expert yoga teacher and is therefore not included in this text.

The neti described here is Jala Neti, that is, the cleansing of the nasal passages using water.

The time for this practice is according to need as well as the weather. For example, if you live in a hot and dry or hot and humid environment or a polluted environment you may have to practise it, maybe twice, both morning and evening on returning home. In case you are staying indoors then only once a day would suffice.

> Note: The practice of Kapal Bhati is imperative post the practice of Jala Neti.

The neti described here is very unique to The Yoga Institute. According to Yogendraji, any other way of practice is being dependent, for example on a pot, and it also uses more water than necessary. Maintaining hygiene and cleanliness of the pot is also cumbersome.

Kriyas are meant to develop self-reliance, develop aishvarya bhava and hence being dependent on props like a neti pot and looking after its cleanliness becomes irrelevant.

Method of Practice

Preparation of Water
1. Take a cup of warm drinking water, preferably boiled and cooled to the required temperature which must be a little warmer than the body temperature.
2. Add a pinch of salt to the water to taste like tears.

Starting Position
1. Wash your hands thoroughly. Stand comfortably, cup the right palm and pour the required amount of the prepared water to fill it.

Steps
2. Holding your palm near your face, close the left nostril with the

left index finger, bend forward to bring the right nostril to the cupped palm. Dip the right nostril into the water and inhale deeply so that the water is snuffed up your nostril and straighten your head.

3. After the water is sucked up in the nostril, immediately bend the head forward and the water will flow out naturally either through the mouth, opposite nostril or the same nostril.

4. Repeat with the other hand and nostril.

Concluding the Practice

1. After the completion of inhaling water through both nostrils blow out gently any watery discharge one nostril at a time. It is necessary that you practise Kapal Bhati after performing Jala Neti.

2. It is important that you do not lie down after the practice.

Jala Neti requires the practice of the following kriyas, but these can be done independently of Jala Neti for their own benefits.

1. Kapal Bhati
2. Kapalrandhra Dhouti
3. Karnarandhra Dhouti (these are described next).

Limitations/Contraindications

Not to practise during severe nasal infection.

Benefits

Physical
1. It improves your eyesight.
2. It cleanses the nasal passages and brings about freshness.
3. It removes all dirt- and bacteria-filled mucus from your nose.

Therapeutic
1. It prevents nasal infections if practised regularly.
2. Bouts of allergies or rhinitis are reduced.
3. It helps to drain the sinus cavities.
4. It reduces the frequency of sinusitis and migraine attack.
5. It helps immensely in pacifying asthmatic symptoms making breathing easier.
6. It helps to prevent tinnitus and middle ear infections.
7. It improves sensitivity of the olfactory nerves, helps in restoring a lost sense of smell and aids digestion.
8. It cleanses the eye ducts and the vision is improved.

Psychological
1. It gives a feeling of lightness.
2. It improves clarity of the mind.
3. When practised regularly irritation and anger get reduced.
4. Ancient yogis used this technique to improve meditation.

Kapal Bhati—The Radiant Face*

*With the head purified, I experience
the luminosity of the intellect.*

The practice of Kapal Bhati has immense benefits. The entire facial region is purified and energized. 'Kapal' is the entire face and especially the forehead. 'Bhati' literally means shining. Its practice brings a glow to the face.

This practice is excellent prior to meditation, as it clears the mind and creates attentiveness.

Method of Practice

Starting Position
1. Stand or sit in any meditative posture, preferably Sukhasana.

Steps
2. Inhale and exhale sharply, forcefully and quickly without contorting the facial muscles. The muscles of the throat will automatically be used. Avoid flaring the nostrils and ensure there is minimal movement in the body.

    The friction created by the sharp breaths will create moderate sounds. Remember they are short, sharp and forceful breaths equal in inhalation as well as exhalation.
3. Practise ten such breaths making it one round. You can practise 3 to 5 rounds.

Note: At The Yoga Institute, vigorous movements of the stomach are not practised. It is done in a way that becomes beneficial to all without any complications.

Limitations/Contraindications
Since there are no vigorous movements there are no limitations. This practice can be done by everyone unless one has been through surgery or trauma.

Benefits

Physical
1. There is a definite increase in lightness and clarity.

2. Blood circulation and oxygenation of the entire face is improved, which in turn improves the texture and gives glowing skin.
3. It rejuvenates tired cells and nerves, keeping the face young, shining and wrinkle-free.
4. This breathing exercise is mainly for cleansing the facial sinuses.

Therapeutic
1. It removes excess phlegm in the sinus and nasal passages.
2. It removes all toxins from the respiratory passages.
3. It improves blood circulation and heart rate.
4. It reduces the frequency of sinusitis and migraine attack.
5. It serves as a therapeutic tool to relieve anaemia.
6. It cleanses the eye ducts and the vision is improved.
7. The sense of smell is improved and aids digestion.
8. The lymphatic system and thyroid function are benefitted.

Psychological
1. This kriya improves concentration. It can be practised before meditation and also by students before they begin study.
2. It brings about a peaceful state of the mind.
3. It helps to relieve built-up stress.

Kapalrandhra Dhouti*

Once the deep-seated impurities, both of the body and the mind are released, I feel rejuvenated.

Kapal, though understood to mean the forehead, refers to the facial region. The term 'randhra' means 'holes' or 'passages'. 'Dhouti' is cleansing. In both the Dhouti practices explained here, the head, especially the face are internally cleansed through an external practice.

Method of Practice

Starting Position
1. Stand or sit erect but comfortably.

Steps

2. Using both hands or one hand, follow the movements as shown in the picture.
3. Make sure you use your fingertips and keep a deep but moderate pressure throughout the practice.
4. Begin by placing your thumbs above the ends of the eyebrows. Using all the fingers, rub your forehead horizontally from one side to the other.
5. Now take your index or middle finger and place it at the bridge of your nose, near the inner eyes as a starting point and move them down under the eyes outwards towards the temples.
6. Rub your index fingers from the front of the ears to the back a couple of times.
7. This practice can be done twice.

Limitations / Contraindications

1. In case of acne, pimples, dry skin or any other problems avoid rubbing the skin but simply go over the said facial area through a press and release motion.
2. In case of very dry skin you can apply a little cream or moisturizer or facial oil before the practice.

Benefits

Physical
1. It is invigorating and energizing.
2. This technique stimulates the facial nerves and the blood circulation to the face is improved. It will render a natural facial glow over a period of time.
3. Massaging thoroughly helps to reduce stress and thereby prevents premature ageing, facial wrinkles.

Therapeutic
1. It cleanses the sinuses.
2. It relieves mild headaches.
3. It calms the nervous system and reduces depression.
4. It has a calming effect on the blood pressure and makes the blood circulate to the head.
5. Migraines are reduced.
6. It helps in insomnia.
7. It aids in prevention of dizziness.
8. It reduces anxiety.

Psychological
1. It reduces stress.
2. It is an effective way for calming the brain and mind.
3. There is clarity of thoughts and calmness sets in.

Karnarandhra Dhouti*

> *The sounds of the universe are divine.*
> *I purify my senses to tune into them.*

'Karna' means ears. This practice not only cleanses the ear canal but also maintains its elasticity and suppleness.

It can be easily done while bathing. Make sure your nails are well-clipped to avoid any injury.

Method of Practice

Starting Position
1. This practice can be done sitting or standing.

Steps
2. Wet your little fingers or index fingers of both your hands and gently insert them into your ear canals.
3. Using gentle movements rotate your fingers clockwise and anti-clockwise in the ear canal. You need not insert your fingers too deeply into the ear canal.
4. Two or three such rotations are enough.
5. Gently remove your fingers.

Limitations/Contraindications
Avoid this practice during ear infections or any other ear problems.

Benefits

Physical
It helps in inner ear blood circulation and clears up excessive ear wax.

Therapeutic
1. It cleanses the auditory canal.
2. It provides suppleness to the ear canal.
3. It prevents age-related hearing loss when practised regularly.

Psychological
1. It has a relaxing and calming effect on the mind.
2. It enhances your focus and concentration.

Jivha Mula Shodhana*

Physical cleansing awakens my mental purity.

The tongue is the repository of bacteria resulting in bad breath, the growth of disease-causing organisms and mental and physical sluggishness.

The cleaning of the tongue is very common for all Indians using a U-shaped silver, copper or a stainless steel tongue cleaner. In older times, a twig of the babul or neem tree was split in half and used as a tongue cleaner. Even today in many parts of India this is quite common.

Jivha Mula Shodhana is cleaning the root of the tongue. This cleansing affects the entire digestive and eliminative processes. This technique is best done in the morning, as it helps a good bowel movement.

Method of Practice

Starting Position
1. Stand in front of a basin.
2. Complete brushing your teeth and cleaning with a tongue cleaner.

Steps
1. Open your mouth wide and insert your index and middle fingers into the mouth and rub the tips of your fingers as far back till the root of the tongue.
2. Continue this rubbing for two to three times till you feel the sensation of throwing up.
3. Gargle with water.

1. No limitations. However, people with hypertension, cardiac ailments, stomach surgeries, pregnancy must use extra caution or may perform this gently using only one finger without any strain on the heart and stomach.

Benefits

Physical
1. It activates all of the taste buds on the tongue.
2. It removes toxins.
3. It reduces bad breath.

Therapeutic
1. The sensation of throwing up results in stomach contraction, which in turn helps in good elimination and reduces constipation (provided you are including a good amount of dietary fibre in your meals and water).
2. It is beneficial in stimulating a sluggish digestion.
3. The tongue is associated with the thyroid, lungs, heart, kidneys, stomach and colon.

Psychological
1. It builds self-confidence.
2. It clears the mind.

Trataka—The Concentrated Gaze*

*Developing one-pointedness and absolute absorption is the
highest aim of yoga.*

Trataka is a kriya with multiple benefits. It has been practised by yogis in different ways not only for its beneficial effects on the eyes but also for improving concentration.

It is also an excellent method to free the mind of all thoughts. When the mind is disturbed, rather than meditation it helps practising Trataka as all distracting thoughts get directed to one non-disturbing focal point.

The mind becomes steady and ready for other practices. A stable and one-pointed mind results in effective management of all actions that we perform in daily life.

Trataka is an intense technique and hence it is cautioned to start for a small duration and then increase the time of practice gradually.

Following are two techniques (cupping and washing the eyes) to be practised after completion of Trataka. You can practise both, but cupping your eyes is essential.

Method of Practice

1. Cupping or Palming the Eyes
    Palming or cupping the eyes is practised after you complete the practice of Trataka. It is a way to relax the eyes after the eye movements. It is also practised after meditation and before opening the eyes. Gently rub the palms to generate some warmth and place the palms on the eyes such that they do not touch the eyes but form a 'cup', shielding your eyes. Hold this position for 5 to 10 seconds. Repeat it according to your need. However, once or twice is enough.

2. Washing the Eyes
    Splashing the eyes with water is common and refreshing. However, you can wash your eyes by taking some room temperature drinking water in one palm and dipping the eye into it for a few seconds. Blink the eye a couple of times when it is in the water. Repeat with the other eye. Rinse and gently pat your face dry. You can also use an eye cup for washing your eyes.
    Variation 1: Bahiranga Trataka Candle or Object Gazing

Starting Position

1. Sit in any comfortable meditative posture or on a chair, keeping your head and body erect. Your hands should rest on your knees or thighs.

Steps

1. Place a candle about two to two and a half feet away from you such that its flame is just a bit lower than the level of your eyes.

In case it is a symbol like a yantra or any other object it must be placed at a similar distance. The point of attention must be as small as possible.

2. Make sure there is no draught of air and the flame is steady.
3. Steadily gaze at either the tip of the flame or the blue light where the wick and flame meet. If you are using an object, choose one point within the object to stare at.
4. Continue staring at the flame till either tears flow from the eyes or the eyes grow weary. Be sure not to overstrain your eyes. Blinking the eyes is a protective mechanism of the body and thus do not stare unblinkingly for long.
5. Now close your eyes and visualize the object or try to see its image within.
6. When this image begins to disappear (it may be anywhere from a few seconds to a minute) cup or palm your eyes and slowly open them.

Note: It is recommended that the room is not brightly lit. It need not be very dark either.

Variation 2: Surya, Chandra, Tara, Graha Trataka

Starting Position
1. Choose a place where you can see either the rising or the setting Surya, which is red.
2. Stand or sit comfortably erect without taking support or leaning on anything.

The other universal bodies you can choose are any phases of the Moon (Chandra), the full Moon, stars (tara) or planets (graha).

Steps—Sun Gazing
1. If it is the Sun you have chosen there will be a small time frame when it will be red.
2. Stare at one point within the rising or setting Sun which is red and not bright. Or, instead of one point stare blankly at the Sun.
3. Once your eyes grow weary, tears come or you wish to blink close your eyes and visualize or see the image within.
4. Gently cup or palm your eyes.

Steps—Other Planetary Bodies
1. In case your chosen objects are in the night sky, stare at it as long as you are comfortable. Be sure you do not overdo these practices, as they may cause harm if you are not used to them.

Variation 3: Hansaji J. Yogendra's Variation

Dynamic Trataka 1

Starting Position
1. Sit or stand near a window, comfortably erect and without leaning or taking support of anything.

Steps
1. Stare into the distance at a faraway object for a few seconds.
2. Bring your focus to a nearby object.
3. Keep alternating the focus from far to near objects for a couple of times.

4. Cup or palm your eyes before you begin other activities.

Limitations
None.

Benefits

Physical
1. It strengthens the muscles surrounding your eyes.
2. It helps in removing tiredness and laziness.
3. It aids in improving your eye health.

Therapeutic
1. It helps to get rid of mild eye problems like short-sightedness.
2. It improves the vision.

Psychological
1. It removes distractions in the mind.
2. It can make the mind calm and steady.
3. It strengthens the ability to concentrate.
4. It improves mental and nervous stability.

Variation 4: Hansaji J. Yogendra's Variation

Dynamic Trataka 2

Steps
1. Standing or sitting near a window, gaze at the clouds or leaves swaying in the breeze or moving objects.
2. Stare blankly at something for a while.
3. Open your eyes wide and close them. Finish off by cupping your eyes.

Limitations
None.

Benefits
This is Hansaji J. Yogendra's unique way of training the sight and the mind to remain focused despite the movement of the object.

It is training the mind not to lose focus in life even though things in the world change.

Variation 5:

Dynamic Trataka 3

Starting Position
1. Sit comfortably in any meditative posture or on a straight-backed chair. Keep your body erect, head straight and palms facing down, resting on your knees or thighs.
2. It must be noted that the entire phases of this variation must be done keeping the head very still and facing ahead. It will only be movement of the eyeballs.

Phase 1—Dakshina and Vama Trataka
1. Keeping your eyes open, gaze straight ahead of you at one point. Slowly, without moving your head whatsoever move your eyeballs to the right shoulder in one slow, continuous movement. This is Dakshina Trataka.
2. Begin moving your gaze to the centre and towards the left shoulder. This is Vama Trataka.
3. Return gaze to the centre point.

Phase 2
5. From the centre take your gaze upwards.

6. Return your gaze to the centre and take it down all the while keeping your head motionless.
7. Return gaze to the centre.

Phase 3—Bhrumadhya and Nasikagrah Trataka

8. From the centre take your gaze to the centre of your eyebrows (cross-look).
10. Return your gaze to the centre and then take it to the tip of your nose, keeping your head motionless.
11. Bring your gaze to the centre.

Phase 4

1. Look straight ahead.
2. Rotate your eyeballs once in clockwise and anti-clockwise directions.

Phase 5

14. With your eyes looking straight ahead try to 'see' the sides, left and right.
15. Finish off by looking into the distance and then close your eyes.
16. Palm or cup your eyes.

17. As you open your eyes blink them a couple of times, open them wide, squeeze them gently and then open them normally.

Note: Once you are used to all the eye movements in this variation you can practise all the phases together.

Though one round of all the above phases put together is sufficient you can practise one more repetition, pausing for a few seconds in between by cupping or palming your eyes.

Limitations / Contraindications
Not recommended for serious eye disorders.

Caution
The eyes are the most delicate and valuable asset of the body. Hence, practise Trataka safely by blinking whenever you feel discomfort. This means not to stare unblinkingly at any external object for a long time.

It must be noted that all eye movements must be non-jerky, and never excessive.

Benefits
1. The ancient yoga texts say Trataka helps in removing tiredness and laziness. It also aids in retaining eye health.
2. Trataka enables increase in concentration.

Agnisara*

> *The all-consuming fire inside, vanquishes the invasions of the impurities I ingest daily and strengthens the core.*

Agni is fire. In this context it is the fire unto which is offered, especially the food we eat. Fire is the vanquisher of all and within this fire all is purified.

Right from the Rig Vedic period, fire was the god unto which all offerings were made. It is the medium through which everything that was offered became purified.

This practice activates the digestive fire.

Method of Practice

Starting Position

1. Stand or sit erect with your hands at your sides.
2. There is no breathing rhythm and no sound as you perform the movements.

Steps

1. Rapidly and forcefully draw your stomach in and then release it.
2. Continue this movement. You can begin with 10 to 20 such movements and increase them to fifty in a day.

Limitations / Contraindications

1. Hypertension, cardiac problems
2. Hernia, pregnancy, any abdominal surgery

Benefits

Physical

1. It tones flabby abdominal muscles.

Therapeutic

1. It improves circulation to the organs of the abdomen, including the reproductive organs.
2. It increases digestive capacities.
3. It reduces stomach gases.
4. It tones, activates and cleanses the digestive and eliminative systems.
5. The functions of the abdomen are enhanced.

Psychological

1. It brings about steadiness of the mind.

Hansaji J. Yogendra's Variations

Variation 1

1. Clench your fist and place them on your abdomen as shown in the picture.
2. Bend forward trying to touch your head to the floor.

3. Rapidly and forcefully draw your stomach in and release it.
4. Continue this movement. You can begin with 10 to 20 such movements and increase them to fifty during the day.

Variation 2

1. Place your palms on your abdomen as shown in the picture.
2. Bend forward trying to touch your head to the floor.
3. Rapidly and forcefully draw your stomach in and release it.
4. Continue this movement. You can begin with 10 to 20 such movements and increase them to fifty during the day.

16

FOREVER YOUNG

The elixir of youth is what all beings seek. No one can stop the onslaught of time, but one can always delay the process and manage it with grace. Yoga and Ayurveda, since times immemorial, have possessed the secret of rejuvenation. In this book, many aspects of yoga have been revealed to make the body healthier, better-looking and the mind peaceful.

The one who practises yoga forever remains young in spirit and body.

In the next few pages, certain timeless techniques have been presented to keep you ever youthful.

GANDUSH—CHURNING WITH WATER

This age-old technique does wonders for your face and mouth. It strengthens your teeth, gums and prevents oral and dental problems. It also improves the shape of your mouth, cheeks and the surrounding skin, keeping it supple and wrinkle-free.

Though traditionally it has been practised using sesame oil, here it has been simplified with using water.

Variation 1

1. Keep two glasses of water ready. One with reasonably hot water (as hot as you can hold in your mouth and swirl around) and the other cold but not chilled.
2. Using alternate temperature water, fill your mouth with water and swirl till the hot water cools and the cold water becomes warm in the mouth.

3. Practise twice alternately with hot and cold water.

Variation 2

1. Fill your mouth with warm or room temperature water. Hold this water in your mouth as long as you can. Your mouth and jaw will begin to feel heavy in half to one minute. Continue for at least two minutes if you can.
2. Spit out the water. Avoid gargling immediately. Relax the mouth.

Benefits

Physical

1. It improves strength of your lower jaw and chin.
2. It improves quality of your speech, voice.
3. It improves the strength of your face.
4. It increases your appetite.
5. It improves your senses of taste.
6. It useful in case of dry lips and increased thirst.
7. It improves the strength of your gums and teeth.

Therapeutic

1. It can help prevent tooth decay as it facilitates the daily evacuation of food debris left in the teeth crevices.
2. It can strengthen the roots of the teeth.
3. It can help prevent toothache as the oil balances and nourishes the nerve tissue and nerve endings.

Psychological
1. It boosts peace of mind.
2. It boosts self-confidence.

FACIAL YOGA

However expensive the creams you may use, nothing can keep your muscles from losing their elasticity as age silently creeps in. The idea is not to remain forever young but to be ever charming and graceful. The different facial exercises presented here do wonders in keeping the facial muscles supple and prevent premature flaccidity.

Practise these exercises daily. They hardly take 5 to 7 minutes and they can be done anytime and anywhere.

Some effective techniques mentioned elsewhere in the book are the practices of Ujjayi Pranayama, Kapalrandhra Dhouti and all the head and neck exercises in the section of Sahaj Bhavasanas.

Benefits

Physical

1. It tones the facial and neck muscles, releases tension and increases circulation to both areas.
2. It improves your complexion and the face looks more relaxed but with firmer contours.
3. It helps in reducing laugh lines and wrinkles.
4. It erases fine lines on the forehead.

Therapeutic

1. It aids in slowing down the ageing process.
2. It releases tension and relaxes the upper part of the body, thus helps relieving headaches, stiff necks and general discomforts.

Psychological

1. It promotes self-confidence, self-esteem and a sense of well-being.
2. You will feel lighter and more uplifted.

STIMULATING THE NERVES INSIDE THE MOUTH

This practice reduces laugh lines, wrinkles and is anti-ageing in effect.

Sit comfortably. Close your mouth and run the tip of your tongue all over the inside of your mouth as described below.

1. Begin with the back of your lips. Slowly cover the inside of your upper lip and then your lower lip. Move your tongue to the right and move it in a circular movement in the inside of the right cheek.
2. Now bring your tongue to the inside of the lower lip and jaw and move the tip of the tongue in that area.
3. Move the tip of the tongue to the insides of your left cheek. Similarly, move the tip of your tongue around in a circular fashion.
4. Run your tongue all around your teeth.

Be sure you swallow whatever saliva that is generated. Swallow it slowly as though you are taking small sips. Do not gargle immediately. This is 'nectar', according to ancient yoga texts.

STRENGTHENING AND TIGHTENING FACIAL MUSCLES

Practice 1

1. As you inhale, pout your lips and take them to the right. Hold your breath and the position for a count of six. Exhaling, return to the centre.

2. Repeat on the other side.
3. Now quickly move your lips from side to side about 4 to 5 times.

Practice 2

1. Keep your lips closed and jut out your chin and lower jaw and move them in and out slowly, inhaling as you push your chin out and exhaling as you bring the chin in.
2. Then move the jaw from side to side for about 4 to 5 times.

Practice 3

1. Open your mouth as wide as you can and move your lower jaw in and out slowly and from one side to the other for 4 to 5 times.

Practice 4

1. Move your eyebrows up and down 4 to 5 times looking upwards with your eyes as you do so.

Practice 5

1. Clench your mouth and smile fully simultaneously widening your eyes. Relax your mouth and repeat the practice five times.

Practice 6

1. Inhaling, pout your lips and extend them. Open your mouth as you exhale. Repeat this practice of pouting and opening your mouth 4 to 5 times.

Practice 7

1. Open your mouth wide, stick out your tongue and move it from side to side. You can sit in the way shown in the picture.

Practice 8

1. Inhaling, look towards the ceiling, jutting your chin out.
2. Exhaling, bring your head straight.
3. Repeat this practice ten times.

Practice 9

1. Turn your head to the right. Jut out your chin and inhaling look up.
2. While exhaling, straighten your head continuing to face right and repeat the practice ten times.
3. Repeat on the left side.

ACKNOWLEDGEMENTS

The Yoga Institute has always believed in an all-round, comprehensive approach to all yoga practices and has continued in this mission. Various asanas, pranayamas and kriyas are becoming popular worldwide. However, the attitude, philosophy and holistic approach related to the same are profoundly missing. This led to the conception of a new book on yoga practices to revive the ancient tradition and experience the unifying power of yoga practices and philosophy. The initial work began with senior teachers from the institute—Harsha Thakkar and Vijaya Magar. The idea of such a book was further strengthened with invaluable suggestions from yoga teachers—Ramendra Jagtap, Ajinkya Meher and Anil Chandran.

To give an in-depth, expression and meaning to my thoughts as well as compile the existing material and render novel ideas of articulating Samkhya Yoga philosophy, Damini Dalal has lucidly elucidated the wholesome nature of yoga in this book. It is a commendable effort to connect millions of people from all over world with yoga and its corresponding philosophy and also to make its practice simple and accessible.

My deepest gratitude to Amitabh Bachchan for the inspiring and encouraging Foreword.

I thank Rupa Publications for ensuring that this profound knowledge reaches out to millions worldwide.

Hansaji Jayadeva Yogendra,
Director, The Yoga Institute,
Mumbai

SELECT BIBLIOGRAPHY

Butera, Robert. *The Pure Heart of Yoga*, Llewellyn Publications, Minnesota, 2009.

Jayadeva, ed. Cyclopaedia Vol. I, The Yoga Institute, Mumbai, 1993.

—— ed. Cyclopaedia Vol. II, The Yoga Institute, 1989.

—— *The Yoga Sutras of Patanjali*, The Yoga Institute, first edition, 2009.

Mishra, Radheshyam. *Handbook of Yoga for Perfect Health*, Yoga Life Society, Ujjain, 1988.

Shri Yogendra. *Asanas Simplified*, The Yoga Institute, Mumbai, 1995.

—— *Yoga Hygiene*, The Yoga Institute, 1991.

Sri Aurobindo. *The Renaissance in India and Other Essays on Indian Culture*, Sri Aurobindo Ashram, Pondicherry, 2013.

White, David Gordan, *The Yoga Sutra of Patanjali: A Biography*, Princeton University Press, 2014.

Yadav, Yogacharya Hansraj. *Yoga Training Guide*, Yogayana, 1987.

Yogendra, Sitadevi. *Yoga Physical Education for Women*, The Yoga Institute, Mumbai, 1934.

INDEX